Of Airships & Automatons:
and Science

By Ross Baxter, Ray Dean, Liam Hogan, Nicole Lavigne, Lee

Parry, Seamus Sweeney, John Walton

Witty Bard Publishing LLC's first Steampunk
Anthology Contains the Following Stories

Detroit's Gain
By Ross Baxter

The Justin Thyme Escape Capsule
By John Walton

Mechanical
By Liam Hogan

The Semi-Modern Prometheus
By Lee Parry

Facing a Modern World
By Ray Dean

An Honest Ulster Spinner
By Seamus Sweeney

Stolen Cargo
By Nicole Lavigne

Detroit's Gain
By Ross Baxter

Running a floating brothel had never been easy, and the meagre profits had often made Bruce Valmont question the sense of what he was doing with his life. But things had started to change. As he pored over the figures again on the adding machine he knew what the answer would be before he pulled the chunky brass handle: for the first time the business was actually making a good profit. Winning the mail contract for Michigan and Northern Indiana had been a master-stroke; the dirigible made the six-day circuit delivering the mail, stopping at a different town on the route each night to furnish clients with liquor and sporting girls. A double-income business that was finally making the money he dreamt about during the lean years. Now, just three weeks after starting the mail contract, the bank balance was no longer written in red ink. Things were definitely looking up.

Valmont decided that he definitely deserved a drink, but on reaching into his desk drawer for a nip of whiskey he found his hip flask empty. With a sigh he rose and headed towards the bar in the public area to replenish it.

"What can I get you, Colonel?" smiled the barman, gently putting down the glass he was diligently polishing.

"If you could fill my flask Tom, I'd be much obliged," Valmont answered with a polite nod. Although he and the men had left the Army Air Corps over four years previously, most still found it hard not to call him Colonel.

While Tom carefully decanted one of the good bottles into the shiny silver flask Valmont looked around at the evening's clientele. The bar was quiet, but from the small number of girls around he knew that most of the rooms were presently occupied.

"Any interesting customers in tonight?" asked Valmont casually.

"The guy over there is a bit loud and drinking like it's going out of fashion, but I don't think he'll be any trouble," said the barman.

Valmont glanced over, quickly appraising the lone drinker. He liked an orderly brothel, and although there was very little his staff could not handle he always preferred to avoid any unpleasantness if at all possible. With a nod to the barman he made his way across to the man's table.

"Good evening sir," Valmont smiled. "I'm the owner of this dirigible and I just thought I'd check that you're having an agreeable night."

The man looked up from his drink, his eyes straining to focus on Valmont. "I am indeed, although you have a poor selection of fine wine. You only stock Californian."

"We find domestic brands satisfy most tastes," Valmont countered.

"Not my taste," the man muttered. "I came aboard to find champagne but you don't have anything even close. I can't celebrate with this slop."

"Well, it looks like you've had a good try," Valmont said wryly, surveying the empty bottle on the table and the remains of a second in a cooler. "What are you celebrating?"

"The end of steam!" exclaimed the man dramatically, sweeping his hand around as if to include the whole of the dirigible.

"That would be a return to the dark ages, sir," said Valmont bluntly.

"Pah!" the man snorted. "We are in the dark ages! Just look at the black clouds spewing from your smoke stack."

"There's no steam without smoke," said Valmont evenly. "And steam is what makes the world turn."

"Well I'm about to change that. You, sir, have the pleasure of speaking to Nathaniel Smock, inventor of Smock's Internal Combustion Engine!"

"I'm afraid I've never heard of it," Valmont mused, extending his hand. "The name's Bruce Valmont. I'm pleased to make your acquaintance, Mister Smock."

"It's Doctor Smock," Smock corrected zealously as he returned the handshake.

"Apologies," Valmont offered, thinking that he should insist Smock called him 'Colonel'. "So, Doctor Smock, tell me how your Internal Combustion Engine will replace the world of steam?"

Smock regarded him as if he was simple. "You won't understand the science, but my engine uses a distillate of oil which is ignited in a cylinder to produce controlled explosions that directly drive the pistons to produce all the power you could ever possibly want. Steam is dead!"

"Surely steam is better suited for some applications," Valmont contended. "Take this dirigible; steam produces both the hot air for the lift and the power for the engines. It's both efficient and effective, how could your engine improve that?"

Smock should his head, derision clearly written across his face. "Speed, that's what! It takes your precious dirigible a week to cover the mail route, a distance my engine could cover in just a day! And as the engine can be made to fit in a small wagon we'll no longer need oversized airships, trains or lumbering steam-trucks. Your precious dirigible will soon be a museum piece."

"But steam uses renewable resources; for every tree cut down in the US two more are planted," Valmont argued. "The whole economies of some states depend on providing the lumber for steam, not to mention the countless coal-mining communities. What would happen to them?"

"They're history!" Smock spat contemptuously.

Valmont leaned back in his chair and studied Smock closely. In his threadbare checked long-coat and yellowed shirt he looked more like a snake-oil salesman than an academic or an engineer.

"So, this Internal Combustion Engine is all your own work?" asked Valmont.

"As good as!" Smock shot back, his face flushing red. "My business partner unexpectedly died a week ago, so I finished everything off."

"So what's with the need for champagne?" Valmont probed.

"I'm on my way to sell the plans and patent to an industrialist in Detroit," replied Smock, unconsciously caressing a battered leather satchel which hung from the side of his chair. "I'm stuck here waiting for a connection; the next train is not due 'till the morning. The town below has no champagne, which is why I boarded your establishment, but which I find is also lacking."

Valmont leaned back in his chair and continued to regard Smock carefully, stroking his greying goatee in contemplation. "Well, I'll tell you what. I'll let you have one of my best bottles of whiskey and the pick of any one of the girls for the night, free of charge."

Smock's bloodshot eyes widened slightly in surprise. "Why would you do that?"

"If you're going to be famous it will be good for business if I can claim the great Doctor Smock as a satisfied customer."

"It will," Smock confirmed conceitedly.

Valmont beckoned the waitress over. "Marian, please bring Mister Smock a bottle of Black Label, on the house. And when he's ready, please introduce him to some of the girls."

"Yes, sir," Marian smiled, winking suggestively at Smock.

****

It was just over an hour later when Marian knocked gently on Valmont's door and slipped inside.

"I've got the satchel you wanted, Colonel," she said, proffering the leather case towards him.

"Thanks," said Valmont. "Will he miss it?"

"Not for a good few hours," she laughed. "After the whiskey

he could hardly stand, and I swear he wouldn't have known if I'd have introduced him to a horse instead of one of the girls."

Valmont opened the satchel and glanced inside. "Good. I'll be with Lou in the boiler-room if you need me."

Marian nodded and retreated, leaving Valmont to swap his expensive frockcoat for the stained cotton overalls which hung behind the door. He quickly dressed, then scooped up the case and stalked aft towards the dark heart of the vessel. One deck later he unlatched the heavy steel door and stepped into claustrophobic heat of Engineering. It was quieter than usual, with only the reserve generator running as opposed to the colossal twin cast iron steam turbines which provided motive power. Over the steady throb of the generator he could make out the sound of heavy hammering and even louder cursing from within the adjoining boiler-room. Stepping carefully over sizzling pipes and oil-soaked thwarts he traversed his way over to the open doorway and the source of the foul language.

"I see you're having fun!" Valmont shouted over the din of the hammering.

Lou Mathabane swung the heavy hammer one last time before rising up from behind the steam duct. Standing over six feet and two inches, she squeezed herself out from beneath an access gantry, nodding a greeting. Sweat poured down her face, glistening like tiny stars against the dark ebony of her skin. Valmont smiled; he remembered having been forced to promote her during the war after his Chief Engineer caught a musket ball in the gut. The decision had caused a storm of protest at the time; not only was she the first female Chief Engineer in the Air Corps, she was also the first Afro-American one. But it proved to be one of the best decisions he had ever made. Not only did she know turbines and boilers inside out, but she had been the first to join him after the war and had proved her loyalty countless times. She also kept the dirigible running on a shoe-string budget with just a couple of stokers.

"You only come to the bowels of the ship when you want something," she growled. "So what needs doing?"

Valmont laughed and held up both palms in admission. "I want you to look at some papers. I need your opinion on their contents."

"Papers?" she asked, raising an oil-streaked eyebrow.

"Engineering drawings. I need to know how viable they are," he explained.

"Sure," Lou nodded, taking a filthy rag from her a pocket in her overalls and wiping the oil from her hands. "Would you care to step inside my office?"

Valmont smiled wryly as he followed, knowing her office was actually just a battered desk at the back of the engineering workshop. Lou pulled up a wobbly stool for him and switched on the sodium lamp hanging above.

"Coffee?" she offered.

Valmont looked at the stained grimy cups on the table and shook his head.

"Let's have a look then?"

He handed over a sheaf of papers. "There's a guy up top bragging about an invention he calls the Internal Combustion Engine. He claims it will make steam obsolescent and change the world, and intends to sell the plans to some industrialist in Detroit to build some sort of powered wagon. I want to know if he's talking bullshit or not."

Lou nodded and perused the papers, opening up and spreading out two large engineering drawings across the cluttered desk. Minutes passed as she looked from the drawings to the typed notes, her eyes flitting quickly whilst her fingers traced over the many diagrams.

"What was the name of this engineer?" Lou asked.

"Smock," Valmont answered. "Or 'Doctor Smock' as he likes to be called."

Lou nodded sagely and continued to read and trace through the sheets.

Valmont waited and patiently looked around the cramped workshop, its walls holding racks of countless tools and the deck littered with boxes full of pistons, cogs and pipes. "No wonder we use so much fuel with all the weight you've got in here," he mused aloud.

Lou ignored him and continued to pore over the papers.

After another ten minutes she finally looked up. "Well, the engineering is sound, as is the science. It would require the cylinder heads to be made from gun-grade steel rather than the brass stated here, and it would need a very specific distillate of oil to serve as fuel, but I think the idea and design is basically sound."

"Could it actually replace the steam-driven engine?" Valmont probed.

"Possibly," Lou nodded thoughtfully. "It would need development, but if the calculations are correct the power to weight ratio of this Internal Combustion Engine is much greater than steam. A much smaller engine could produce much more power than a steam turbine."

Valmont stared silently past his Chief Engineer, his mind considering what she had imparted.

"I don't really think that this Smock character did the work," Lou offered. "He seems to have crudely erased the name of the author on every page and replaced it with his own. It looks like the drawings and theoretical calculations were actually done by someone called Miller. Miller or maybe Milner, some name like that."

"He claimed his so-called partner had died," said Valmont.

Lou shrugged. "What are you going to do, steal the plans?"

"No," he replied. "We've been virtually broke since the war. It's taken us four years of hard graft, but finally we've secured the mail contract for Michigan and Northern Indiana, and for once we're starting to make real money. But we're still paying off the loan on the dirigible and the last thing we need is to lose the contract to a faster vessel or a powered wagon. We simply can't afford the death of steam."

"What then?" asked Lou, a look of puzzlement written across her broad features.

"I'll return Smock back to the ground, and by the time he sobers up we'll be long gone," he answered.

"What about selling the plans to the industrialist in Detroit?" probed Lou.

"I've a premonition that Detroit won't miss the Internal Combustion Engine," said Valmont firmly, sweeping up the papers and dropping them onto the glowing coals in the small tool furnace behind him. "Long live steam!"

The Justin Thyme Escape Capsule: Commonly referred to as 'The Joey'

By John Walton

The Justin Thyme Escape Capsule was the brain child of one Padraigh Kelly, and his associate, Rear Admiral, Royal Imperial Air Navy {Australia}, {cashiered}, the Right, not so Honourable, Bertrum Wattlecake.

Why the 'Justin Thyme' and not the 'Kelly-Wattlecake'? To find the answer we need to look into the skies over that far away continent, Australia, and cast our minds back to the year 1855.

Padraigh Kelly was an aeronaut turned skyway-man, the first of that breed of desperado. He was an inventive individual to be sure and, having found no outlet for his active imagination as a young orphan pressed into the Air Navy, he had turned his talents to crime. It is true that crime itself is hard work; Padraigh never shirked from hard work. It was the shackles and lashes that society meted out to one in his position that he would not take. He broke free.

He was successful at his endeavours until the fateful day he met and fell in love with Sarah Grist, and, she with him. In an effort to save him from a probable early death, she advised the constabulary as to when and where Padraigh's next robbery was to take place. Needless to say they nabbed him and his equipment and took the credit for the detective work.

The police, who by necessity to do their work are devoid of imagination, did not notice the potential that his device offered. It was stored, as custom dictates, for return to him when he was to be released five years later. Australia, with no colonies of its own had nowhere to send him. It fell to the Australian Government, or more accurately, its citizens, to support Padraigh on his sabbatical.

Wattlecake, on the other hand, was from a good family, and well respected in the colony. He was being groomed for high political office when a certain discrepancy in campaign contributions was noticed. To avoid a scandal his family purchased him a commission in the R.I.A.N. {Australia}. He was resolute in his duties and rose in the ranks. A note on his file always warned his superiors to make sure he was not entrusted with the administration of any monies.

The war of secession in the United Kingdom offered him a chance to show not only his strong sense of duty but his valour. His dashing exploits, heroic defences, glorious retreats and stylish surrenders made him the nation's darling.

On his return, Wattlecake was promoted from a position where he was, happy, fulfilled, and successful, to that of a flag rank political stooge. The dizzy heights of this new rank put him above any application of the warning note on his file. Boredom played its part. His devious, deceitful nature, such an advantage in battle, now served him again.

By careful manipulation of movement orders, a new airship, already paid for but never built, was constantly on patrol, especially at audit time. When he required more funds, he added another imaginary airship to his fleet. As the years progressed he eventually had an entire squadron.

The reports filed by him, supposedly coming from what must

have been the hardest working squadron in the Navy, attracted the interest of the Colonial Governor. This individual, a political creature to the core, was ever eager to ride to glory on the efforts of others. He announced that he wished to 'Honour these gallant fellows.' To cut a long story short, Wattlecake, eventually had to admit that the heroic fleet did not, in fact, exist.

Wattlecake was disgraced, cashiered, and sentenced to three years hard labour. The most heinous crime he had committed, of course, was to have embarrassed the Colonial Governor. The judge made it clear that any payments or manoeuvring to ease his time in custody would result in a similar fate for any who helped him.

It was here in the New South Wales lockup two years later that he was joined by Padraigh, and here that the next step in this journey began.

The new cell mates could not have been more ill matched and at first they took an instant dislike to each other. Padraigh, an armed robber and ne'er-do-well from the second lowest class imaginable: a person with convict parents (the actual convicts being the lowest class). The Aboriginals did not count as they were still considered by law to be animals. Wattlecake, on the other hand, was from the direct opposite end of the class spectrum, but, no less of a scoundrel.

They discovered that they shared two things in common. After swapping a yarn or two in the long cold nights they discovered their kinship. They were firstly, both aeronauts, and secondly, too clever for their own good.

Padraigh was explaining his modus operandi to Wattlecake one day and this set Wattlecake to thinking.

Padriagh's method was to board a long-flight airship as a paying passenger. Long haired, with an eye patch and ferocious whiskers, his was a face to be remembered. He would have a large steamer trunk containing: a parachute, a new and frighteningly dangerous piece of equipment, only to be used as a last resort; a folding bicycle, see previous remarks; the usual paraphernalia of an outward-bound prospector; and a brass-framed Stoom-en-mampoer revolver, the dragoon model.

During the flight he would befriend his fellow passengers with his easy charm and gain entry to their cabins for a look-see. He would then wait until they were far enough from civilisation and late on the chosen night he would sneak into the hold and prepare his escape equipment: folding bicycle, parachute and revolver, with saddle bags fixed firmly to the frame of the bicycle for the swag. The bicycle would then be concealed on the deck for easy access and exit.

On the stroke of midnight Padraigh would cut his hair, shave his beard and moustache, remove his eye patch, don a black silk hood and proceed to enter the cabins of his chosen victims. If occupied and awake, the presentation of a lethal revolver kept things quiet, the application of chloroform even quieter. If the occupants were asleep, they slept a little sounder. His last call would be to the captain and a quick looting of the ship's safe.

Once the spoils were transferred to the saddle bags he would leap astride his bicycle, pedal furiously through the gangway gate, and out into the wild blue, currently black, yonder.

The parachute would deploy and he would land gently enough, on terra firma, swiftly pack the chute away, pedal off to the nearest town and make his way to the train station.

By the time the stupefied victims had come round there followed some minutes of wailing and gnashing of teeth, the cries of 'I've been robbed', 'Where is the villain?' etc. The captain calmed the passengers and had the roll called. Mr Smith was missing. The captain, crew and passengers then proceeded to make a thorough search of the vessel. He was nowhere to be found. The conclusion was that he must have gone. Overboard!

By this time they had no idea as to where and when he had departed the ship. This resulted in further delay in alerting the authorities by a message drop. Mr Smith, now safe and comfortable in his first class compartment, was on his way home.

Wattlecake wanted to expand the concept, and together they came up with a contraption that would allow a team to escape after the robberies where complete. It would also float, so that the much more lucrative cruise airships could fall prey to their scheme. The plans were kept in their heads, to avoid discovery by the guards. As it is human nature to misinterpret, many a heated debate arose when the time came to construct the machine. Serendipitously they were to be released one week apart.

On gaining his freedom Wattlecake put his family contacts to good use and selected Geoffrey Sternfrett, the least pleasant of his uncles. Geoffrey refused to speak with him and Wattlecake was forced to use a more direct method to gain an audience. He broke into Geoffrey's house late at night and cornered him in the bedchamber.

Wielding a poker, Wattlecake launched into a heart-rending plea for funds. Such was his eloquence that it only required a couple of prods and a gentle tap on the head from the poker to persuade Uncle Geoff to hand over 2,000 pounds, the deeds to a town house, and a shakily written letter to his tailor instructing him to fulfil all of Wattlecake's requests, however bizarre.

Wattlecake set up his establishment and on the appointed day sent a hackney to collect his new partner.

They first took time to taste the fruits of freedom. Unfortunately, this used up the generous cash advance from Geoffrey. A second attempt at tapping Uncle Geoff revealed that, not only had he employed a couple of bully boys to guard the entrance to his home, the lights stayed lit all night and, from the looks of them, starved mastiffs roamed the grounds. Wattlecake was at the same time both flattered and annoyed.

Padraigh was of the mind to do one quick flying visit to Alice Springs and on the way drop down with some ready cash. Wattlecake insisted that until they were ready for the big ones they would go straight. Padraigh. for his part, said that this was not in their original agreement and that he lacked or had forgotten the required skills.

A council of war was called to assess their dwindling assets. They had: themselves, the house and its fixings, and the tailor's account. Wattlecake was on familiar ground here, and advised his associate that the servants would soon leave when the pay dried up, but, two well-dressed gentlemen living at a superior address could garner credit, at least for a short while. This gave them time to plan and organize and to await an auspicious time to set out on their project.

The scheme worked well, planning was done during the periods of rest between: whoring, gambling, attending the theatre and meeting the duties of swells about town.

Purchasing on credit and a bank loan or two to cover necessities, they continued in this fashion for a further six months. The auspicious day came when, with no servants and a crowd of creditors howling for blood outside the front door, it was deemed the correct time to depart for points west, destination: Woomera the Royal Imperial Air Navy {Australia} Aerostat base.

They worked their passage on a commercial airship. Wattlecake, blessed with a strong mannish tenor, as a singing barman, and Padraigh at his old trade, Able Aeronaut.

The plan was for Wattlecake to impersonate a high-ranking Air Navy officer and set up a secret operation in a remote corner of the aerostat yards. Thus, they would have workshops, labour and supplies at a cost to suit their pockets.

After relaxing for a day or so they set their plan in motion and set themselves up in the taproom of the Royal Woomera Molly House to wait for a victim, one of the many aeronauts who frequented this establishment. The Molly House was referred to far and wide as the RWMH. or the house of Raw: Whisky, Meals and Harlots.

Wattlecake and Padraigh had just finished their meal when four crewmen on liberty from a patrol airship out of Perth arrived. A rowdy cheer to the bar girls for service and company had the barman send over to their table a tray of drinks with a couple of the house ladies.

Determined to get drunk in the shortest possible time they finished the drinks in a record swill. By the time the third rod had arrived they were well on their way. Their good humour and generosity soon attracted more house ladies to their table, each one attaching herself to one of the aeronauts as her own.

The band had started up and added to the din, one of the aeronauts staggered up to the band and in a loud and near unintelligible slur demand and that they play the 'Tony Hoom song... shanty... thing.'

After acknowledging the free drinks, the band set to with a will and thundered off in a cacophony of guitar, didgeridoo, snare-drum and vocals with the popular 'Boom Tone Wizard'.

As the song ended the band, and indeed, by this time, half the taproom, yelled the closing chorus:

He's a boom tone wizard

He's got the lot

He's a boom tone wizard

he'll tie you in knots

With a crashing, final almost-chord, the band raised their drinks in salute to their benefactors.

The crew at the table had now hit their stride and were in for the long haul. One young man had been dancing on the table and ended up on the floor, his mates picked him up; he was unhurt and soon in of arms of one of the capable ladies of the RWMH. Our heroes did not have long to wait until one of the roistering crew headed up the back stairs with a blowsy redhead.

Padraigh finished his drink, left the table and walked purposefully towards the back stairs. Once at the top he listened carefully to identify the room from which the grunts and languid groans emanated. He opened the door a crack, and yes, there they were. The aeronaut's clothes a heap on the floor and he a heaving heap on the bed. The molly had her eyes tight shut and was making the moans of her profession with gusto. Padraigh thanked his luck and swiftly entered, scooped up the clothes and closed the door quietly behind him. He exited out of a passage window and dropped into a noisome alley behind the Molly house.

At their lodgings he changed into the borrowed clothes. Now dressed as an AA, Able Aeronaut, from the AS "Zeefer Winds" out of Perth, he proceeded to the Land, Sea & Air Officer's Equipment and Apparel Store. He presented himself and said that he was come from the Admiral Justin T Thyme, The Right Honorable Earl Gray, with an order.

Wattlecake had assured Padraigh that the Admiral was regarded highly in Air Navy circles and in society in general. Thus it proved, and Padriagh was granted an audience with the head tailor. Padraigh stressed that the Admiral had not yet arrived but expected everything to be ready when he did so, in two days time. He handed over a set of measurements from their tailor in Sydney. The head tailor, seeing the note paper as additional proof of his new customer's status, promised to deliver as ordered. Padraigh also informed the tailor that the Admiral's mission was of the top-most secrecy. No one was to be told, not even the captain's superiors, and under no circumstances contact the tailor in Sydney. He added that the Admiral's successful conclusion of the mission would bring the tailor wealth, fame and longevity

The order was for: firstly, a set of uniforms, including working rig and full mess dress for the Admiral; secondly, for himself, outfitting appropriate to his rank, but befitting his position; thirdly, two sets of civilian clothing each, as they were to be working incognito.

The order placed, Padraigh returned to his lodgings and changed back into his worn clothes. At the Molly House he tossed the borrowed uniform into the alley and entered to find Wattlecake still sitting quietly at their table.

The uniforms duly arrived and, now resplendent n the full fig of an admiral, Wattlecake sallied forth with his trusty manservant to bring about the next part of the plan.

On arriving at the naval yard, Wattlecake demanded of the

sentry an audience with the duty officer. Ignoring, as one of his rank is wont to do, the pleas for identification he simple raised his voice and repeated his wishes. As the volume increased with each exchange the nervous and now confused guard did as he was bid.

When the officer of the watch arrived, it was to see Wattlecake established in an office with tea and biscuits, whilst his man stood guard at the door with a fierce protective stance, the official guard having retreated to his post at the gate. Padraigh, on seeing the officer of the day arrive, leapt to attention and ushered him into the oh-so-august presence of his master. Captain Stanley was impressed and when he learnt of the identity of the Admiral and was eager to do his bidding. Wattlecake explained that he was on a hush, hush, hush mission and that once he had finished with the good Captain he would not return until all was ready and then not as himself but as a civilian. Captain Stanley was quick to presume that association with the Admiral would lead to swift promotion and a glorious future.

The captain was nervous and the Admiral complimented him on his military mind and his sagacity. He then had Padraigh produce from his coat an envelope that had obviously come from the Air Navy's highest echelon.

It had contained the results of Wattlecake's courts martial and dishonourable discharge. Now it contained a letter claiming to come from the desk of the Air Navy Marshal, ordering all who read it to follow the bearers' instructions without let or hindrance. It was signed and sealed with a squiggle and a smeared red mess of wax.

The damage had been done with the presentation. Wattlecake had informed Padraigh that none of the captain's rank would recognise the Marshal's signature or his stamp anyway, and so it seemed, for the captain was immediately at his most helpful.

What he required, explained Wattlecake, leaning in conspiratorially, was the following:

1] A workshop in the yard with a rear entrance, unguarded, locked and away from the main gate.

2] A work team: carpenters, sail makers, artificers, wheelwrights and coopers.

3] An open order on the stores.

4] The captain was to come see them at the Royal Woomera Molly House in four days' time and escort them to the workshop, by which time all would have been done.

5] The guard unit on detail must immediately be replaced and sent to New Guinea for a year's posting, to await further orders and to be instructed to do nothing but mingle with the locals and to act as ambassadors.

All hush, hush, hush, said Wattlecake, with a wink and a finger laid alongside his long nose. For further incentive he added that the reputation of the Air Navy, for initiative and decisive action in emergencies, although flagging at present, showed signs of renewed vigour in the person of Captain Stanley.

Four days later the captain arrived and led them to a hastily constructed gate at the far corner of the Navy yard. It opened into a walkway roofed and sided in corrugated iron, already pinging in the early morning heat. This led to the work shed where the team was ready to begin work on the building of the very first multi-seated escape vehicle.

Wattlecake first dismissed the Captain then turned to the team and told them that each member would be promoted one rank, and assured them that hard work would be rewarded by hard cash, as the purse strings of the Air Navy were connected to this project. A draughtsman was seconded, and once his drawings completed, sent on holiday.

They all worked at a frantic pace. Both Padraigh and Wattlecake knew that they could not keep up this subterfuge for long, and drove the team hard, day and night.

At last the work was complete and the vehicle was ready for shipment. Captain Stanley was contacted and advised that a steam train was required to move the prototype to its new, secret destination.

The fortunes of Wattlecake and Padraigh had also improved during this period by the simple expedient of selling some of the materials through the back door, however, this lead to their downfall.

An audit had been called to question the sudden drain on the store. Captain Stanley, whose job now seemed to consist of deflecting eyes and ears away from his clandestine crew, forestalled them with the hint of the hush, hush, hush work being carried on.

Unfortunately the eagle-eyed auditor pointed out that the amount of material being sent to the workshop, unless it was being destroyed, would now represent a stack larger than that of the workshop itself. He also pointed out, that a number of the new houses in town had been made from lumber with Air Navy stencil markings.

Captain Stanley desperately pooh-poohed the idea, saying that the auditor was not looking at the problem as an experienced military man. It was well known that once the Air Navy had its hands on something, it could simply, disappear. Into thin air. Poof. Like that. And no reasoning or measuring could bring it back. Just so, said the auditor, and he was now determined to go and check out this ready-to-hand example, to better understand the process, as it were.

The captain, now at his wits' end (and true it had not been a long journey), invited the auditor to accompany him the next day for an interview with the man leading the hush, hush, hush operation, believing that the august presence of the renowned Admiral would bring an end to this inquiry.

The next day Wattlecake and Padraigh, arriving early, as was their wont, found that the night shift had left and the day shift had not clocked in. Their feral instinct for survival kicked in. They grabbed what they could and fled. Amongst the items they took were two bicycles. The need to travel fast was essential. They hid the bicycles at the north end of town and bought two tickets for Perth on the Airship leaving that morning. Then they went and hired two horses from the livery stable.

They rode directly east and after an hour's hard ride stopped at a small shack village. It was easy to hire two men to ride the horses. They were told to continue east for five days. After that they could keep the horses but were warned that they could expect a call from Woomera.

These men, being of a particular quality advised, "No worries mate." They assured they would leave a clear trail, would not be caught, and that the horses would disappear, converted into cash, by the magic of the land.

Wattlecake and Padraigh waited till dark and made their way back to the bicycles and pedaled off to parts unknown.

Meanwhile back at the Woomera Air Navy Aerostat Yard, Captain Stanley and the auditor arrived at the shed to find it deserted. The captain surmised that the operation, now awaiting only transport, was complete and that the men had been laid off. It was after all very hush, hush, hush you know. If fact it was so hush, hush, hush he was not sure that they shouldn't just leave it as it was. Let sleeping dogs lie, so to speak.

The auditor grunted that it was more likely to be lying dogs, and that they were not sleeping but had legged it.

The contraption in the workshop held little interest for the auditor; it was a piece of machinery, and therefore the province of labourers, artisans, engineers and the like. But, paperwork, documents, journal entries, that's what mattered. He searched the untidy desk the waste basket and rummaged in the fire place. He did not mind getting his hands dirty, as long as it did not involve machinery.

He found a bundle of papers containing: inventories, list of parts, assembly instructions, blueprints, what looked like loaders' tally sheets, a name and an address. All added up to shipping orders for material to be sent to the new estate of, and here he exclaimed out loud, - Lord Gray, Admiral, Justin T Thyme. A glance at the captain's face told him that he had discovered the name of the mysterious man in charge, a name that the captain had steadfastly refused to tell him.

This of course put everything in a new light. It would need careful handling, being no longer theft, but politics. He knew that Lord Gray was soon to become the First Admiral of the Fleet, a position so close to God that it could possibly make the post holder blind, if not insane. He advised the captain that he was aware of the Admiral's special mission, and, if the captain had but mentioned the Admiral's name, none of this current investigation would have been necessary.

He needed to speak to the men involved, and told the captain to leave them in no doubt to their future. To ensure Captain Stanley delivered the correct message, he enumerated: 1. Stripped of rank, 2. A year in the glass house, 3.Transfer to The Ice, the Antarctica penal infantry battalion, 4, Any who survived their enlistment, would receive a dishonourable discharged, without pension. He added that they should consider, pretty sharpish, anything they would like to say in mitigation.

The captain gasped, and grasped at the proffered straw; the auditor was taking over, as of now. This left the captain in a happy and familiar place that of simply following orders. The last two months had taken their toll. He had found himself, in the early hours of the morning, adding beer to his whisky so the final bottle could last until the commissary opened. He now had an inkling of what the words combat fatigue could mean.

Interviews revealed that the men had overheard some mention of the contraption being used to escape from airships. An engineer called in to examine it said that he could understand the principle. Though how someone had made such a leap of faith as to actually construct the dammed thing, based on such a foolhardy idea, he could not fathom.

Actually, now that he had the device in front of him, he was prepared, with reservations, to admit, that it might work.

What they really needed, he said, was for some volunteers to try it out. The work party who had been nervously awaiting their fate, and understanding military-speak, volunteered to a man. Plummeting to their deaths accompanied by splintering wood, twanging lines, ripping canvas, a cloud of dust and finally a tinkling of attachments, was not too hard a pill to swallow considering the alternative. And, it might work.

Before we take to the skies on the test flight let us have a look at this contraption that gave the engineer pause for thought.

It was a long tube mounted low on a carriage frame, resting between a set of four strange looking wheels. It was fourteen feet long and five feet wide, wheel hub to wheel hub. The wheels topped the cylinder by six inches and were seven feet in diameter. The body, or cylinder, was made out of the light and strong Chinese wonder wood, bamboo. Long lengths lay on a hexagonal bamboo frame, bound at intervals with strengthening hoops of copper. Along its length, on both sides, were a series of brass-framed portholes.

On each side of the cylinder, between the fore and aft wheels, was attached a wing, This was made of a bamboo frame with waxed cotton stretched over it. The wings could be retracted and stored along the sides of the tube. At the rear were two horizontal tail fins and a taller vertical fin of the same construction as the wings. Mounted on the top of the cylinder's front and rear were two wicker boxes. These contained the parachutes made of the strong compressible silk cloth, attached with silk cord risers.

The top section of the cylinder swung open along its length, hinged on the port side. The interior was padded in quilted cotton and down the centre were a number of canvas seats. Each seat had a set of leather straps to secure the occupant. On the floor at each seat was a set of pedals. There was space for up to ten people to sit tightly packed one behind the other. The pedals rotated a crown gear; this acted against a worm gear and turned the main shaft, which ran fore and aft for the length of the cylinder. It passed through a gland to the forward bulkhead where it connected to a basic gearbox offering only forward or reverse. The gear box drove two side shafts that transferred the pedal power to the wheels.

The plan required that this device be used on both land and water. This was why the wheels looked so strange. Each had a set of paddles integrated into the spokes, allowing propulsion through water.

The pilot's compartment, later to become referred to as the "Suicide Seat", was at the bow and consisted of an open cockpit containing the controls. It was sealed off from the rest of the craft, except for a speaking tube that connected the pilot to the interior. The tube had a tightly fitted cap and a ball valve to prevent water entering the passenger compartment.

The controls were simple. A column with a set of bicycle handlebars mounted on the top. Push forward and the wings contracted, to speed the fall, pull back and the wings extended, to glide. Turn left, the vehicle would veer left, turn right and she would go right. There was a gear shift for forward or reverse and a parachute release handle. The instruments consisted of a compass and an altimeter. A leather helmet and goggles hung over the handlebars to welcome the pilot.

The concept, alluded to in the scattered paperwork, gleaned from the workmen's scuttlebutt, and deduced by the engineer, was this: in an emergency the crew of an airship would climb into the contraption. The pilot would seal them in and take his place in the cockpit. At his command, the crew inside would begin to pedal and the escape pod would race over the deck and out over the side.

Once away from the mother ship it would begin to fall. At this point the engineer proposed that the front be weighted to ensure that it would fall nose first. The pilot would extend the wings to slow down or retract them to speed up. His limited steering would give some sort of control over destination.

Once the contraption was headed in the correct direction and they were close enough to land, the pilot would pull the large, red parachute release handle. The lids of the wicker baskets at the front and rear would fly open and the parachutes would be released.

These would slow the vehicle down and swing her horizontal for a survivable impact on the independently sprung wheels or, in the case of a water landing, on the hull. The wings would also assist as stabilisers in the case of a water landing.

The auditor immediately placed all involved incommunicado. He contacted Admiral Thyme via coded telegraph. The auditor correctly deduced that the best way to protect the Admiral, whose name had been misused, would be to recover his honour, and the Admiral could of course reward the auditor for his swift action to protect it. As the Admiral's name had been used to have the thing built, then he should take the credit. It was poetic justice of the sort that appealed to both the auditor and to the Admiral.

The suspense-filled test flight had been held in secret and was successful, much to the relief of the volunteers. The new device was declared 'Fit for Purpose,' and the plans received the official rubber stamp.

The "Justin Thyme Escape Pod" was introduced to the world, and the Admiral emerged as a great humanitarian. This new engine of his would save countless aeronauts lives. Also, with the ever increasingly popularity of air tours, the operators could now add safety to the enticements offered to paying passengers. The workmen were well compensated and sworn to secrecy; the Admiral's embarrassment was now hidden, and the fame was his.

But, this is not the end of the tale. There were rumblings amongst the crews of the airships. Rumours spread, and the truth leaked out. It was said that it should have been called the 'Kelly-Wattlecake' escape pod. Yet another case of the kudos floating inevitably to the top, where the powers that be lay like scum on a cesspit. To crush this mutinous talk, Lord Grey, now First Admiral of The Fleet issued a general standing order.

To All Vessels and Installations, Royal Imperial Air Navy

"If any person or persons, knowingly, or unknowingly, have dealings with individuals or groups supporting the unfounded rumours regarding the origins of the "Justin Thyme Escape Pod", OR, they themselves aid in the spreading of these seditious rumours. They will be guilty of treachery, NO appeal. Sentence to be death, by being cast from an airborne aerostat."

By My Order on This the 15th Day of June in the year of Our Lord Eighteen Hundred and Sixty-Two

Lord Grey, First Admiral of The Fleet, Justin T. Thyme.

Nos Possident Aetheres -- We Possess the Skies

As is so often the case, this did not produce the desired effect. A new name appeared in the 'tween-decks slang, ''The Joey', author unknown. It encapsulated the newness of the idea and its Australian origins, and mimicked the way in which the device was carried about by the parent airship. It also hinted at a rebirth of the occupants.

In emergencies it came to supersede the more clumsy full title. Attempts to call it a "Life-Carriage" were ignored by the crews, and the Air Navy, with a legacy of thousands of years of man management, let it end there. Except for senior government executives and officers, when in an official capacity, where the "if we ignore it, it will go away" and the "we are always right" attitude prevailed along with the official name. However, to everyone else it was the Joey.

Carousing junior officers, and midshipmen in their cups, called it the Joey. Officers began to realise that use of the new term, when on station, resulted in happier crews and a rise in moral. This was noticed, and then implemented, in the leadership training courses, so that the term, "Justin Thyme Escape pod", was soon relegated to the plans and drawings only.

As an end note, the names of the two real inventors, that of Padraigh Kelly and Bertrum Wattlecake became a rallying cry, and synonymous with the emerging social revolution.

Mechanical
By Liam Hogan

"Knight to B4" von Kempelen said, his English only slightly accented.

The itch on the end of my nose was getting worse but I ignored it, just as I ignored the urge to lift the edge of the blindfold. My hand still smarted from the last attempt and if I hadn't been promised payment I'd have jacked it in, then and there. My stomach rumbled, this stupid game had gone on far too long.

"Bishop to E5—revealed check." I replied. I could hear the wooden piece clacking down to its new home on the board, and a half grunt from my opponent.

"King to—"

"C7?" I interrupted. "Unwise. Knight to D5—checkmate. Your best move is pawn to B3, but it will cost you your queen. You should have taken the exchange when you had the chance."

"My, you are the impatient one. Still, you may remove the blindfold, Miss...?"

How little they thought of me to forget my name already! "Haley." I said as I pulled away the strip of dark cloth. "Sarah Haley, and I believe you owe me a half-crown, Herr von Kempelen."

I had not expected the lazy smile with which this was met with and my fingers almost flew to the blade I kept hidden in the lining of my coat.

"All in good time," von Kempelen drawled. "Tell me, Miss Haley, what is your height?"

"My height?" I coughed "What the devil..."

"5 foot 2, wouldn't you say Mister Doyle?"

Mr Doyle spoke for the first time since he'd blindfolded me. "5 1, Sir, and either ninety-three or ninety-four pounds. I'll stake a shilling on it."

"Well, you're the expert Mr Doyle." von Kempelen said. "Mr Doyle was a hangman, and a very good one, before he found his way to me. You know how a hangman judges the weight of the condemned?"

I shuddered, as I remembered Mr Doyle's firm hand shake. "Now look..."

"Calm yourself Miss Haley. Mr Doyle, a half crown if you will. But if you want more—a half crown a day plus food and lodgings, then come see me tomorrow, at five o'clock."

I caught the coin as it flew across the smoky room, but I didn't move, not yet. A girl has to put up with a lot to make it in this world, and I preferred the games to remain firmly on the chequered board. "Is this about the Turk?" I asked, defiantly.

"Ah!" von Kempelen grinned. "It seems our reputation precedes us, Mr Doyle."

Of course it did. The Mechanical Turk was the sensation of the day. I'd learnt about it from my father, God rest his soul, but back then it was reported irreparably broken, until it had reappeared over the Channel in Paris a little under a year ago. And now here it was, newly arrived in London!

"If you're going to ask me to play against the Turk, Sir," I said

"I don't need to come back tomorrow to decide. I'll gladly do it."

"Good girl!" von Kempelen smiled. "You'll take my pay, then, and come into my service. But there are two things you need to know. The first, is that my business is my business. I will not stand for loose talk, and the disclosure of the secrets of any of my inventions will not go unpunished. You can, I trust, keep a secret?"

"I can. If the pay is regular?"

"It is." He held out his hand, and I looked at it suspiciously. He had yet to tell me the other thing I needed to know. Still... a half crown a day was a persuasive argument, and I assumed we would go no further unless I agreed. I shook.

"And the second thing?" I asked, our hands still joined.

His smile stretched from ear to ear. "Why, Miss Haley, I don't want you to play the Turk. I want you to be the Turk!"

****

I suppose it should have been obvious, the Turk, the chess-playing automaton, the mechanical wonder of the century, was a fraud. A very clever one, but a fraud none-the-less. The clockwork mechanisms did little but mask the fact that there was still space enough for an operator contained within. It took me a while to master the controls—the magnetic counters on the underside of the chess board, the shielded lamp so that I might see the levers and pulleys for the Turk's arm and head. I had to learn to move swiftly and silently from compartment to compartment, while the innards of the Turk were revealed to the audience before each game, the wooden panels opened to show light all the way through. I learnt from Pierre, a homesick Frenchman whose trembling frame and pale white face belied a fierce intelligence, the only man I could never beat on the chessboard. But he was a broken man, I heard him whimpering in his sleep at night and the way his hollowed eyes kept darting to the doors and windows as if looking for an escape, for a desperate return to the wife and kids he oft talked about, had me doubling my efforts to master the Turk's operation.

While I learnt, I was paid nothing but board and lodging, the half crown withheld until I was fit for the job for which I had been employed. My door was kept locked at night, excused with a smile by the ever present hulking Doyle. Still, I wouldn't have missed it for the world. I attended every performance, watching the way the crowd gasped and shrank back the first time the metal arm moved, the way they laughed when the Turk shook his head as he corrected an illegal move. I learnt von Kempelen's polished spiel, the explanation for the Turk's robes and turban, the "traditional costume of an oriental sorcerer" he proclaimed, all the while masking the true origin of the smoke from the lamp by which Pierre operated.

At last, I played von Kempelen once more, this time as the Turk, and, evidently having performed to his satisfaction, was told that the next day I would finally take Pierre's place.

I'd have expected Pierre to be happy—surely this would mean he'd be able to go home—but he just gave me a weak half smile and retired early for the night, rubbing his bony back and not even playing our customary evening game.

I won't go into detail of that nerve wracking first session, the way the smoke sometimes escaped into the compartment making my eyes water, the cramps, the slow build up of heat, or the fact that for the last hour I played with something sharp sticking into my side. Despite it all, I emerged into a grey dusk, giddy with excitement at having played and beaten so many men, men who would otherwise never have deigned to play against a mere girl of seventeen years. I was sure I'd played the best chess of my life. I'd played aggressively, and won, freed from the obligation to not show up my male opposition, freed from the fear of retribution. A heady feeling that evaporated when I saw the patch of blood soaking the dark shirt I wore. Doyle's eyes lit up when he saw the injury, but von Kempelen was quick to reassure me. "We'll have that fixed immediately—it must be a loose strut. The Turk needs constant maintenance, constant repairs. Where were you when...?"

I pointed vaguely into the Turk's dark interior, though in the area I indicated there was no metal work to be seen. "Perhaps Pierre...?"

"Pierre is no longer with us." Von Kempelen said.

I looked at him, surprised. "I... he's not?"

"He boarded a packet boat for Calais after watching your first game. It seems he was more than happy with your operation, my dear."

I flicked my eyes between the pair of them, but Doyle's were back to their impassive norm and von Kempelen's piercing gaze held no clues as to why he was lying. You don't live by the Thames all your life without learning something about the tides.

"You will be fit to play again tomorrow, I trust?" von Kempelen said, with a note of the imperative.

I nodded. "Of course."

****

Sometime during the long night, my sleep destroyed by dark dreams; dreams of armies of mechanical men, men clothed in turbans and cloaks, wielding sharp blades, I thought I heard voices, thought I saw a light briefly appear and disappear, felt a draught stir the stale air around my bed.

"You said you'd fixed it!" one voice said.

"I did" a tired voice replied. "These are not... the same."

"How can that be?"

"I don't know. I just don't know. I thought after Pierre..."

"We can't go on like this!"

"Can we not? Operators are cheap and with each, the Turk gets stronger. Besides, this is as much out of my hands as yours. Blame the Emperor, if you must, but never forget that somewhere out there, there is a hangman ready to measure both of us up for what happened in Vienna."

****

That was the last time I saw the Turk, or von Kempelen, or mercifully, Mr Doyle. They really should have realised that someone who could fit into the Turk's small compartments, might find a way out of their lodgings, other than via the secured door.

I slipped out an hour before dawn. Trembling in the cold, my coat and other winter clothes left behind, I traded my necklace for a place on the coach to Oxford and from there walked the eight long miles to Abingdon, where my Uncle, a book maker, lived. It was hard to leave London, harder still to become little more than a menial drudge at my Uncle's beck and call, keeping as low a profile as I could manage.

"Didn't you used to play chess?" he asked, one day. "My brother..."

I shook my head vehemently. "No sir, I was never any good at it."

"A pity," he said. "It would have at least shown a spark of intelligence. Might have got you married and out of my hands. Though who'd take a frail, dull thing like you, I don't know..."

****

I stayed until I heard the news that the Turk had left England, destined for Leipzig. My Uncle laughed when I asked where Leipzig was, his laugh fading to a puzzled stare when he saw the broadsheet in my hand. The dolt still assumed I couldn't read, though I'd been fixing up his mistakes since the day I'd arrived.

I left him the next morning, heading back to London, to the printing houses there, a forged letter of recommendation and my ink-stained fingers as references. I changed my name and played the wide-eyed girl in London for the first time.

For a while, I followed the news about the Turk as it toured the European cities, wondering when it would be exposed. It never was though, not even after it had returned to Vienna and the news fell silent. Even so, I never dared reveal the Turk's secret, or return to the chessboard that I loved so much.

I suppose von Kempelen still owes me a half crown, now I come to think about it, for my one day as the Turk. But I'll waive that gladly, in return for my life, and for my immortal soul.

The Semi-Modern Prometheus
By Lee Parry

Three-Card Braggart

A bloke being shot dead over a game of cards wasn't anything new. It was just that it usually happened in some seedy pub in some seedy part of town, not on some swanky high-flying airship.

Not that Kwame Asseri, escaped slave and professional ne'er-do-well, should have even been on the SS Indefatigable. His ticket had been 'inherited' from a gentleman unable to make the flight from the mountaintop hamlet of Shirehead to Three Pines.

To describe Kwame as a fish out of water would have been both clichéd and entirely accurate; the only black man on an airship filled with monied nobles, he had already garnered his fair share of sideward glances. Nevertheless, a black man had almost never held a ticket for a dirigible flight, first class or otherwise, but the purser had, despite his best attempts to keep the clearly troublesome individual off the ship, ultimately failed.

Kwame had been seated — with no small amount of consternation — at a table with a coal magnate, two Portstown nobles, a self-styled gentleman scientist and a horseless carriage merchant. After the evening meal the ladies, as was customary even at twenty thousand feet, retreated to the drawing room to speak of whatever it was women spoke of, whilst the gentlemen remained for brandy and cigars.

"Horselesses shall always be necessary in the confines of a city, Your Grace," continued Johnson, the horseless carriage merchant. "Portstown more than most, but even the Pines has need of them. Rest assured, the influx of coin shan't waver."

"From a scientific viewpoint, these new trackless locomotives are fascinating," said the gentleman scientist, a man by the name of Avery Goldsworth. "The details are lost on the layman, of course, but the use of gyroscopic suspension is really quite inspired."

"Tell me, Mister… Asseri," said the second of the nobles, a podgy young man by the name of Lord Randall Grosvenor, "have you ever chanced to journey in a horseless?"

Kwame looked at the man blankly for a long moment.

"Aye, Your Lordshipfulness. Believe it or not, Petat has a fine line in horselesses and the like."

There was a nervous chuckle.

"What an absurd question, Randall," said Duke Whitworth with a chuckle. "I shouldn't imagine a technological marvel such as Petat even has truck with such base steam-powered antiquities as horselesses any more, what?"

"Oh, aye, it's all sunshine and dreams up there," said Kwame, draining his brandy and calling for another. "The gods' own people, they are. Have a wee trip up there, Your Majesty. They're no big on provincials so ye might get some stick, like, but I'm sure ye'd enjoy it nevertheless."

"'Your Majesty' is the correct title for the King," said Randall coldly, laying his hand on the table. He wore a single leather glove; the underside was dotted with circles of smooth metal. "You shall address me as 'My Lord'."

"Sorry about that," said Kwame casually. "I've a lot tae learn about your civilised ways down here."

"How is it, Mr. Asseri," said the coal magnate, a Mr. Frederick Barlow, "that a Petatian Negro finds himself in the Mire?"

"The Petatians aren't averse to making a freedman of a fellow, if he proves his worth," said Duke Whitworth smoothly. "I'm sure Mr. Asseri here is as valorous and brave a fellow as has ever been freed from Petat."

"Aye, there's that. Or ye could even murder ye master an' turn runaway," said Kwame with a grin. A fresh brandy arrived.

"Ah," said the Duke, his smile faltering. "Well, I'm sure that wasn't the case with you, Mr. Asseri."

"Let's hope not, eh?" said Kwame, sitting forward and making several men flinch. "Wouldnae want an escaped murderer on your nice wee airship here. Imagine the talk."

"Quite," said the Duke, glancing at Randall. "Shall we have a friendly hand of cards, gentlemen?"

"Aye, I could do wi' lining my pockets," said Kwame, rubbing his hands together.

A deck of cards was brought. Barlow took the new deck and began to shuffle them with a practised hand.

"In three-card brag, Mr. Asseri," began Barlow, "every player is dealt three cards —"

"Oh, aye?" said Kwame, raising his eyebrows. "Thass why they call it 'three-card brag', is it?"

Barlow looked at the Negro coldly.

"Believe it or not," said Kwame in a hushed voice, "I know how tae play three-card brag."

"It's quite a complex game. I'd be happy to recap the rules."

"I'll muddle through." He leaned back, and Barlow glanced, not for the first time, at the gleaming pistol strapped low on the man's thigh.

Each man was dealt five hundred's worth of thick bone chips. After five hands Kwame had around seven hundred in his pot, largely at the expense of Lord Grosvenor and Avery Goldsworth, who had admitted to not having much of a head for cards.

"It's not the probabilities I have a problem with," said Avery, his waxed moustache somewhat dishevelled after an hour of hard spirits. "I'm quite accomplished in mathematics. It's more this... bluffing malarkey. How am I to name a man dishonest? The height of... hic... rudeness, what?"

"All in good faith, isn't it?" said Kwame, lifting his new hand up slightly. "Not as if we're actually cheatin' each other or anythin'."

"Dishonesty comes quite easily to certain people, hmm?" said Randall, looking at Kwame coldly.

"I like tae think I've a flair for it, Your Honour."

"I'll wager you've used that honorific on a number of occasions in your time," said Randall, his wavering gaze not leaving Kwame's. He finished his brandy, some dribbling down his fleshy chin, and called for another.

"My Lord, that's quite a weapon you have there," said Avery, slurring his words only slightly. "May I?"

"Of course, Mr. Goldsworth," said Randall with a thick-lipped smile. He pulled his pistol from the holster with his gloved hand and offered it grip-first.

"Wonderful craftsmanship," marvelled the scientist, turning the slender pistol around with a look of awe. The weapon gleamed silver; two small cylinders containing miniature electricity coils cleaved to the underside of the barrel. "A rail pistol, no?"

"That's right," said Randall, his smile broadening. "That beauty is capable of putting a bullet through ten men, if you've a need for it."

"In my experience, blokes dinna tend to arrange themselves in a line before ye shoot 'em," said Kwame.

"I shouldn't imagine your experience extends to such expensive firearms," said Randall.

"Ye're no wrong. I make do jes' fine wi' this'un." Kwame patted his own sidearm. "S'a nice piece, though. Why's it have wee coils?" he reached over, only for Randall to snatch it back.

"It's complicated. Physics and such. You wouldn't understand."

"Aye, I'm a thick bastard. Do all right wi' cards, though." He dropped his hand and looked pointedly at Randall's diminishing pile of chips. "How are you goin', cob?"

"I'm reaching the limit of my tolerance for your insolence, Negro," snarled Randall, jamming the pistol back into its gold-inlaid holster and launching himself to his feet. "In Portstown, our blacks know their place."

"Randall —" began the Duke, raising his hands.

"Is that right? S'pose I'm lucky we're no in Portstown, eh?" said Kwame, leaning back and grinning.

"Just one more word, Sir —"

"Ach, fuck off," said Kwame with a dismissive wave. "Sit down an' play ye hands, eh?"

The two nobles and Barlow gaped at him, their mouths outraged O's.

"You dare —"

"Bloody animal!"

"I demand satisfaction!" snapped Randall, slamming his hand down on the table. "I shan't be spoken to like that by any man alive, let alone a subhuman such as you!"

"Don't half get their knickers in a twist, eh?" said Kwame, nudging the perfectly drunk Goldsworth, who really was quite enjoying the whole fiasco. "Ye want me to buy ye another brandy or wha'? Touchy bastard."

"You misunderstand me, Sir," said Randall grimly. "I challenge you to a duel. Forthwith."

"Oh, a duel," said Kwame. He considered this and shrugged. "Aye. All right. Fleecin' ye at cards was beginning tae bore me anyway."

"You might reconsider, Sir," said Goldsworth nervously. "That pistol really is worth the money it costs —"

"Ach, the day I canna beat some chubby toff in a firefight's the day I want puttin' in the ground anyway," said Kwame dismissively.

"Name your second," said Randall, his face almost comically serious.

Kwame hesitated. "My wha'?"

"Your second, buffoon, your man."

Kwame shrugged. "I dinna swing that way, myself. Not that I'm surprised tae find out you do —"

"I shall second for him," said Goldsworth quickly, as Randall's face became apoplectically red.

"Very well. Your Grace, may I count upon your support?" said Randall, still looking at Kwame.

"Of course, old chap," said Whitworth with a thin smile, patting Randall's back.

"I shall see you on the aft deck in an hour, savage."

Randall stormed from the dining room, the Duke in tow. A moment later Johnson and Barlow exchanged glances and left after hurried good-byes.

"Mr. Asseri: I fear you misapprehend the situation. Did you, perchance, espy the peculiar gauntlet our noble acquaintance was sporting?" said Goldsworth.

"Is there nae a bloke speaks the King's fuckin' English round here or wha'?" said Kwame exasperatedly, throwing chips into a napkin. "Is the dictionary compulsory bedtime readin' round here or somethin'?"

"Allow me to rephrase: the glove His Lordship was wearing on his right hand. Did you see it?"

"Aye. Weird get-up, all shiny circles on it. Presumed it was some weird sex toy or the like." Kwame took Goldsworth's chips without much protest.

"Uh… no," managed Goldsworth. "It's paired with the gun. When a charge passes through it — activated by our corpulent friend — the gun shall leap from its holster and into his hand. It's much faster than a traditional draw, I'm afraid."

Kwame considered this.

"So the fat bastard's gonna be fast," he said with a shrug. "So wha'. I'm nae slouch myself."

"I hope so. The technology is really quite fascinating."

"The hole I put in the chubby fucker's head's gonna be quite fascinating." He stood up and nodded at Goldsworth. "Cheers for, uh, 'secondin'' me or whatever ye call it."

"Not a problem, Sir. You're far more interesting that the other blowhards around here," said Goldsworth with a chuckle. "And please, call me Avery."

"Might stick tae callin' ye 'cob', if it's all the same. Avery's a bit of a poncey moniker, eh?"

"It's possible I'm not reading the dictionary enough," said Goldsworth slowly.

"Never mind. Probably best not knowin'."

***

They met on the aft deck, the polished oaken planks exposed

to the elements. The captain — an acquaintance of Lord Grosvenor's — had taken the dirigible down from the thin high-altitude air to accommodate the duel, and the choked green forests of the Mire were visible through scudding clouds.

Randall Grosvenor was already on deck, practising his quick draw as Duke Whitworth looked on approvingly. Kwame had to admit — he was fast. Grosvenor would extend his right hand, flex slightly, and the pistol would leap from the holster and into his hand as if by magic.

"Nifty," said the Petatian. "Hopefully the fucker can't shoot straight."

"I do enjoy your colourful vernacular, Mr. Asseri," said Goldsworth with a smile.

"Cheers, possibly," said Kwame. "So how's this work?"

"His Lordship shoots you, you die. I arrange for a coffin."

"Brilliant. What happens before that?"

"Well, the two of you shall stand back to back. You shall then walk ten paces. When the signal is given, you turn, you draw, you shoot."

"Right."

"Just try not to hit me, Mr. Asseri."

"Call me 'Kwame'. Since ye're my coffin man, I'd like tae think we're on first-name terms now."

"Very well, Kwame. I should add, Sir, that we don't all share those fools' sentiments regarding fellows of colour. It's a shame that in this day and age, we are still unable to see past the colour of a man's skin."

"Aye, it breaks a bloke's heart." Kwame raised his voice. "You ready, Your Magnificence?"

"Indeed," said Randall with a smug smile, holstering his pistol. "Don't worry; I shall make it fast."

"Bet your missus has heard that a few times."

Randall reddened.

"Backs together, gentlemen," said Duke Whitworth; as the challenger's second, he was in charge of arbitrating the duel.

Kwame and Randall stood back to back in the middle of the wide deck. Quite a crowd had gathered.

"On my mark, gentlemen; ten paces. Go."

The two men did as instructed. The Duke held up a handkerchief.

"Three; two; one…"

The Duke dropped the handkerchief.

"TURN!"

The rail pistol leapt from its holster before Kwame had cleared leather, and he could see he'd lost.

Randall smirked and squeezed the trigger.

Kwame closed his eyes and waited for the bullets to slam into his body, but nothing came.

"Confounded thing!" snapped Randall. He squeezed the trigger again; the gun gave a sad little phut and a flash of light, but nothing else happened. "Bloody ridiculous! Fire, dammit!"

"So can I still kill him, or wha'?" said Kwame to Avery.

"Well, technically, but —"

Kwame pulled his gun and shot Randall twice. His gun was back in the holster before His Lordship's body had hit the floor.

"Cheers, fellas," said Kwame, nodding to the Duke and Avery. On the deck, a surprised Randall died without much ceremony. "Brandies're on me, if anyone fancies."

Kwame gave the crowd a little wave and went back inside.

Murder Most Recidivous

A knock came at the door of Kwame's swanky first-class door early the next morning; he gave a groan and pulled himself up.

"Aye, aye, giz a sec!" he said irritably as the insistent rap came again. "Glom's bollocks, knockin' a bloke up at the crack ae dawn…"

He pulled the door open to the nervous face of one of the sailors.

"Wha'?"

"There's been a killin', Mr. Asseri."

"Aye, I was there. Fucker had it comin' and it was all legal, like, so dinna be tryin' tae drag me off tae the brig or anythin'."

"Eh? Oh, that. Won't find many of the lads too bothered about that dickhead's passin'," said the airman with a rough chuckle. "Nah, s'a different bloke been seen to. That scientist bloke's askin' for ye."

"Goldsworth? Fuck's sake…" He pulled his trousers on.

"Kwame? Where are you —" came a woman's voice. She lifted her head and her face fell as she noticed the sailor. She pulled the sheets up and gaped at the airman in shock.

"Dinna you worry, sweetheart. Gentleman scientist bloke jes' needs my expertise."

"Lady… Grosvenor?" said the airman, his own face a picture of shock.

"She was overcome wi' grief at her husband's passin'," said

Kwame, buckling his belt. "I stepped in. Did the gentlemanly thing."

"You say a word," said Lady Grosvenor, her colour high, "I'll have your job."

"She will, an' all," said Kwame with a chuckle.

"I won't say a word, Milady. O' course not."

"Right, Ye Ladyship. Sympathies for ye loss an' all that. I'll see ye later." Kwame closed the door behind him and buttoned his weskit up. "Where's Goldsworth, then?"

"You bedded the man's widow?" said the airman with something approaching admiration.

"Ach, she couldnae be happier her fella snuffed it. A mansion an' half a million sovereign, an' no chubby tosser lordin' it over her? I should murder a noble every week. My cock'd never be dry."

***

"This flight doesnae lack for eventfulness."

"Indeed." Goldsworth was peering at the corpse's mutilated face; the man's left eye had been plucked out with no small amount of delicacy, but only after he'd been beaten severely. Purplish blotches had bloomed on his stomach and chest, and his throat was wreathed with thick, purple-reddish marks. "The captain asked me to take a look. I've no small amount of expertise with criminology, as well as my considerable abilities in the other sciences."

"Wank yerself off in your cabin like everyone else, Avery.

Wha's this tae do wi' me?"

"Oh," said Goldsworth, taken aback. "Well, ah… you seem the sort of chap to have experience with this sort of thing. I thought you might lend me your expertise."

"Aye, aye. You ask me, some bastard beat the shite oot ae him an' had his eye out."

"Yes… well, sort of self-evident, isn't it? The question is 'why?' I've to interview the people he was talking to last night. I was wondering if you'd care to help me?"

"Why me?"

"Your command of the playing-card game last night, for one. You have a knack, Sir, for spotting a lie."

"Aye, all right. How much're ye payin'?"

"Paying?" Goldsworth looked nonplussed. "Aren't you intrigued, Kwame? The brutality of it! A murderer walks amongst us, Sir, and it is our privilege — nay, our duty — to track him down and see justice done!"

"Aye, justice is great an' all that, but I dinna work unless someone's slingin' some coin my way."

"Why, that's…" Goldsworth sputtered and his brow beetled. "How cold-bloodedly mercenary of you!"

"Aye. Key word: 'mercenary'. Sortae my job."

"Well, what else are you going to do?"

"I can think of at least four things, an' only one ae 'em doesnae involve reamin' a recently bereaved widow. So let's see some coin, or I'm off."

"'Reaming' a — egads, man, have you no shame?"

"I'm no rich enough tae afford shame. You payin' or wha'?"

"Fine, fine, bloody hell. I've a small research stipend. I suppose I can give you some of that."

"Brilliant. Who's the corpse, then?"

"A merchant by the name of John Downes." Goldsworth took a magnifying class and peered closely at the bloody eye socket. "Removed with some care… whoever our killer is, Sir, he's no small amount of skill with a blade."

"Wha' makes ye think it's a bloke?"

"Of course it's a man. The savagery of the attack… the removal of the eye… a woman has neither the physical wherewithal to enact such an attack nor the medical knowledge to remove an eye so carefully."

"For such a learned bloke, ye're very quick tae write off half the fuckin' species as limp-wristed simpletons," said Kwame, peering at the purple bruises on the chest. "I've met many a lass vicious enough tae twat a bloke up an' surgical enough tae make it hurt like fuck."

"You propose the murderer is, in fact, a murderess?"

"Could be. Who was he with last night?"

"The passengers seated with him last night are awaiting our questions." Goldsworth peered at the socket again. "Why take the eye?"

"Some sick fuckers out there. Treat killin' like a sport, some ae 'em. Like tae take trophies."

"Repeat killings. Some kind of… recidivous murderer?"

"Tae coin a phrase."

"The door was locked. Whoever did it had access, or knew the victim." Goldsworth glanced back at the body. "I suggest we interview our suspects before anything else."

***

"So, ah, Mr… Davies." Goldsworth gave a tight smile and consulted the sheaf of paper before him. "You were dining with Mr. Downes last night?"

"Aye, I were." Mr. Davies was a big, gruff man with rough hands and the red nose of a habitual drinker. "Bit of a poncey bloke, but he were all right."

"'Poncey'? What do you mean by that?"

"Ye know." Mr. Davies shifted uncomfortably. "Scented handkerchiefs, frilly shirts. Poncey."

"You mean to imply that Mr. Downes was a homosexual?"

Mr. Davies stared blankly. "Ye what?"

"A bender," said Kwame helpfully.

"Oh, right. I dunno. Jus' know he drank tea instead o' whiskey an' talked like you."

"I… see." Goldsworth's pen scritch-scratched on the paper as he avoided acknowledging Kwame's toothy grin.

***

"And what's your purpose on the airship, Mrs. Collinson?"

"I'm taking my husband home," she said with a glassy smile.

"Really? You're travelling with your husband?"

"That's right." Mrs. Collinson, a portly lady with pallid skin and a moist handkerchief clutched in one hand, gave Goldsworth another brittle smile.

"I see…" Goldsworth clucked his tongue pensively and tapped his sheet. "Here's the thing, Mrs. Collinson… there's no record of your husband in the passenger list."

"Ah… yes." She smiled again. "Well, you see —"

"Ye're nae with ye fuckin' husband, are ye?" bellowed Kwame, slamming his hands down on the table and causing the woman to start. "Why ye lyin' tae us? What've ye got tae hide?"

"He's not on the passenger list!" she shrieked. Tears started to spill down her pale cheeks. "He's not on the list because he's — he died!"

"Oh, he died. Another poor bastard on ye death list? Ye seduced the poor fucker and then beat the shite ootae him like sick murder-gorilla, didn't ye, ye murderous cow —"

"He died! In Shirehead! A mining explosion! I'm — I'm taking him back to Portstown for burial, don't you see?" She sobbed lustily into her handkerchief. "He's in my chambers because — I can't bear to be parted from him! Please!" She broke down into keening wails.

"Oh… yes," said Goldsworth nervously, tapping a sheet of paper. "Here he is. Mr. Collinson, deceased." He glanced sheepishly at Kwame. "He's listed as, ah, 'cargo'."

"Oh." Kwame straightened up and considered this. "Right. Jumped the gun a wee bit there, didn't we?"

"I miss him so much…"

"Aye… I'm away for a pint, Avery." He patted the scientist on the shoulder and opened the door. "I'm no half shite wi' criers."

***

"He was really quite knowledgeable about biodiversity in the Mire, you see. We spoke for some time."

"Oh, aye?" said Kwame, stifling a yawn.

"Indeed. There's a particular genus of creeper…"

"This fella didnae do it," whispered Kwame.

"How can you be sure?"

"I'm not, but I'll be fucked if I'm listenin' tae this shite for another minute." Kwame looked up at the man, now waxing lyrical on a rare strain of pond algae. "Right, cheers for your time, pal."

The man stopped, nonplussed. "But I was talking to Mr. Downes just before he went back to his room. I should think my testimony indispensable —"

"Aye, we'll be in touch if we need anythin' else," said Kwame, taking the man by the arm and rushing him out of the door.

"Much more ae this, I'll be strangling myself."

"I should say we're no closer to finding our killer, Kwame."

"You take a breather, Avery. I'll handle the next one."

***

Goldsworth sighed and put his pen down.

"Well, it seems we're not getting anywhere. Between our

botanist, the remarkably short-sighted alcoholic fellow, and your traumatising of a grieving widow and a seven-year-old boy —"

"— That fucker's hidin' somethin', I'm tellin' ye —"

"— I'd say that we haven't a single suspect."

"Far as I'm concerned, every one ae 'em's a suspect."

"Right." He sighed again. "Well, I suppose we'll go back and interview them. Catch them in their quarters."

"Well, crack on. If we dinna sort it out we'll be in the Pines, and then we'll never catch 'em. Oh, an' do me a favour." Kwame took a package out of his pocket and tossed it to the scientist. "Have a look at this."

Goldsworth opened it, inspected the contents, and glared at Kwame. "Does your larceny know no bounds?"

"Apparently not, since I've no the first clue what 'larceny' is. Jes' fix it."

Enticements of Science

Kwame rapped on the door. Five hours in, and he was already tired of the detective game. The amateur botanist had bored him almost as much as last time, banging on about lichen. Too boring to be a murderer. He'd not bothered with the kid.

That brought him to the widow, with her glassy smile and the dead husband in her cabin.

He was about to knock again when the door opened a crack. It was dark and gloomy within, and Kwame couldn't see anything except for her red-rimmed eyes and pale face.

"Mrs. Collinson?"

"I've already answered your questions, Mr. Asseri, I have no idea what else you could possibly —"

"Jes' routine follow-up questions, Mrs. Collinson. Sorry about all that carry-on earlier. We've tae be thorough, ye know how it is."

"No, I don't!" she said, as Kwame pushed the door open and walked in. She stared at him open-mouthed. "Do you mind?"

"Need a quick look around. Eliminate you from our inquiries, sortae thing," he said, his eyes adjusting to the gloom.

The cabin's curtains were drawn closed and there was little in the way of light. He could make out the coffin on a stand at the foot of the bed. Several of the dressers had been pushed together and their surfaces stocked with an array of scientific equipment. Kwame was only marginally better with science stuff than he was with criers, but he knew a rat corpse when he saw one. The large grey-white thing was splayed on its back, its belly slit open and held there by long pins. On either side of it were miniature electrical coils. To one side lay another mutilated rat.

"Weird set-up for a grieving widow, eh?"

She looked at him blankly. "What do you mean?"

"All this science shite."

"My husband was a scientist," she said, clutching her handkerchief to her bosom. "I assisted him quite often in his experiments."

"So what's this all about?" he walked over to the splayed rat and prodded it. In the gleaming viscera of its belly were several black stitches.

"My husband was a surgeon. He experimented with organ transplants."

"Well, thank the gods someone was finally standin' up for the wee rats."

"Animal experimentation is a necessary precursor before moving onto human beings. He… he was close to a breakthrough. And his work shall never be finished unless I pick up the slack."

"So where were ye after dinner last night?"

She sighed. "This again? You think me capable of murder?"

"Anyone's capable ae murder, under the right circumstances. Where were ye?"

"I was here, of course."

"Can anyone back ye up?"

"Only my poor Henry." She stared forlornly at the coffin.

"The dead bloke can corroborate. Case closed, then." He looked at the coffin. "How did he die?"

She wiped at her eyes absently. "A mining explosion."

"I thought ye said he was a surgeon?"

"He was touring the mine."

"Right. Explosion… bet he's a right fuckin' mess, eh?"

She blanched.

"Yes."

"Mind if I have a wee look?"

She gasped. "What?"

"See what kind of damage we're talkin' about here."

"Of course not! First you accuse me of murder, and then you come here quite uninvited and barge into my chambers —"

There was a flurry of quick raps at the door. Mrs. Collinson glared at him furiously and opened the door.

Goldsworth was standing there, panting.

"There's been another murder."

"Wha'?" He looked at Mrs. Collinson suspiciously. The widow's face was flushed with shock. "When?"

"Just now. Not ten minutes ago." He glanced at Mrs. Collinson. "This would better be discussed en route to the scene."

"Aye, they might be even more dead if we dinna crack on." He glanced at Mrs. Collinson suspiciously. "I'm onto ye, lassie."

She gaped at him again. "I was here with you!"

"Aye. It's a clever trick, usin' me as your alibi, but —"

"Kwame, if you've quite finished harassing grieving women…" said Goldsworth exasperatedly.

Kwame wagged a finger at the widow.

"Dinna think this is the end of it. You an' all your weird science. I've got ye number, pet."

"Get out, you foolish man."

"What've we got, then?"

"An airman. Beaten, strangled, and his stomach opened up. One of the poor soul's colleagues overheard, went into his cabin, and took a nasty blow to the head for his troubles."

"The stomach? She's gettin' sicker by the second."

"Would you shut up about the widow? She was with you when it happened."

"Ye shoulda seen her chambers. Like somethin' ootae a penny dreadful."

"Her husband just died. She's bound not to be acting rationally."

"Did ye see that shite? Cut-up rats, electric coils, and her husband's bastard body in the room with her. She's no right."

"Electric coils?"

"Aye. On about transplantin' organs or some shite."

"Hmm." Goldsworth frowned.

"Wha'?"

"Hmm? Oh, nothing. Let's concentrate on this fresh corpse."

"When I walked in, Geoff was already down. His eyes were bulgin', stomach all cut up already," said the airman, an ice pack held to the back of his head. "Then someone clocked me. I couldn't have been out of it for too long — a minute or two. When I got up, he was gone."

Goldsworth knelt next to the body, peering at the wound. "A good portion of the intestines are gone."

"Jes' like her fuckin' rats."

"Egads, man, you'll hound that poor woman straight into the same grave as her husband."

"Look, ye soft-heeded shite," snapped Kwame, glowering at the scientist. "She's a bunch ae dead rats in her room. Both ae 'em cut up. She's taken the guts from one and stitched 'em up intae the other. Ye think it's a coincidence?"

"But… she was with you when the attack happened. And the injuries… she's not strong enough, Kwame, I'm telling you."

"An accomplice might be."

"Accomplice?" Avery frowned. "She booked onto the ship alone. She's friendly with no one. Who could her accomplice possibly be?"

"I'll tell ye one thing I'd wouldnae mind knowin'. How much damage did that minin' explosion do tae her husband?"

"Yes… there's something awfully queer going on."

"Let's go an' have a word with her. Before more folk start turnin' up less their innards."

"Mrs. Collinson!" Goldsworth rapped sharply on the door again. "You must open this door, Madam! This is a matter of the utmost urgency!"

"You ain't half soft as shite, Avery. Outtae the way."

"What?" Goldsworth turned to look at the man. "We've no warrant, Sir! No legal pretext to —"

"I dinna do legal, cob," growled Kwame, his face solemn.

He lifted his booted foot and slammed it into the door with all his might.

"Ow! Ye fuckin' cunt, ye."

"Look on the bright side. I believe you scuffed it slightly."

"Ach, the fuck away wi' ye." Kwame pushed him aside, grabbed the handle, and slammed his shoulder into the oak door.

It only took him seven or eight barges before the stubborn door finally gave in and flew open.

"Are you all right?"

"Aye. Reckon I'll have feelin' back in my shoulder as soon as tomorrow," replied Kwame sourly, massaging his upper arm. Goldsworth went in.

"Extraordinary," said Goldsworth in hushed tones as he peered at the rat corpses. "She's quite accomplished, our grieving widow. The sutures are quite seamless."

"Aye. She's fuckin' wonderful, for an unhinged lunatic," said Kwame, ambling over to the coffin.

"These resonant transformer circuits… astonishing."

"Resonant wha', now?"

"The electric coils. Now why, Kwame, do you think she might have a dissected rat between two transformer circuits?"

"She's a sadistic cow?"

Goldsworth face became apprehensive. "Open the coffin."

"Aye." Kwame grasped the heavy lid.

He stared into the shadowy recesses and raised his eyebrows.

"What?" said Goldsworth anxiously, coming towards him. "What is it?"

"That's jes' it." Kwame nodded at the interior. "There's nobody here."

There was a noise in the doorway.

"You shouldn't be here."

Thy Adam

They both turned to look. Mrs. Collinson was in the doorway, her pallid face grim.

"An' ye shouldnae be fuckin' around wi' deed bodies, love, but it hasnae stopped you."

"Shut up!" she hissed, her face flushed and her eyes still red-rimmed. "What would you know of it? Of my husband's work?"

Kwame's hands strayed to his pistol. "Ye'll wanna be showin' us ye hands now, pet."

"I tried my best," she continued obliviously as she walked in. "I tried to continue his work. For him, you see? Not just for his memory... for him."

"Seriously. I'll put one through ye fuckin' heart if I dinna see them hands."

"Give her a moment, Kwame," said Goldsworth, holding a hand up. "What do you mean, you did it for him?"

"I had his transformer circuits shipped with us," she said, her eyes darting around the room. "The big ones."

"And where are they, Mrs. Collinson?" said Goldsworth nervously.

"He never perfected the technology, of course... even fresh rats only came back for a minute or two... but the neurological deterioration was negligible. They were almost as before, really. More or less the same."

"Mrs. Collinson: where are the transformers?"

"It doesn't matter. Doesn't matter," she said with a shake of her head. "He was… too far gone. Missing an eye, half his bowels gone… I couldn't fix him. I tried, but how he howled… how he howled." Her red-rimmed eyes fell on the coffin. "I just put him back."

"He's nae in there."

She gaped. "What? What are you talking about?"

"I fear that… something went awry with your experiment."

"No." She shook her head again. "No, it's impossible. I —"

"Are ye dense or wha', lass? Ye wee science experiment went tits up an' ye've unleashed a mental undead lunatic. He's had an eye oot an' now he's had some poor bastard's guts for garters, so ye'd best start talkin'. Where the fuck are these transformer things, an' what else does the bastard want?"

"I —"

"Just one more thing. My love."

Their heads snapped to the door.

"The monster is nothing. Without his heart."

The three of them stood stock-still, transfixed by the sight of Henry Collinson in all his returned glory.

He was still clad in his funeral suit — a dark tailcoat, high-collared white shirt and waistcoat — but it was now spattered with blood and viscera. His skin was grey and blotched, and one eye had begun to cloud over.

The other eye was bloody and fresh, however, and seemed to stare out from the explosion-torn flesh of his face at something quite different from the cloudy one. There was something like terror in that eye.

Collinson's shirt bulged at the belly, as if he had a paunch. It was only after a moment that it became clear what it actually was: guts, stinking and fresh, piled in and sutured.

A steel box, thick with pipes and clockwork, was affixed to his chest. It pulsed with bursts of electricity.

He held out a hand.

"Come with me. My love. Be with me. Forever."

"I said it was like some shite penny dreadful, didn't I?" said Kwame as he jabbed a finger at Goldsworth. "Fuckin' undead electro-corpses shamblin' around the place —"

"For once would you shut the hell up and shoot the bloody thing!"

"Nooooo!" screamed Mrs. Collinson, and she lunged at Kwame as he drew. The bullet bounced off the wall, and he swore, drawing a fist back to swing into her face —

Collinson was on him. The thick stink of the grave crowded his mouth. Kwame took a cold fist to the chest, and another to the head. A moment later Goldsworth was sailing through the air, hitting the coffin and tumbling to the floor with it.

"Oh, Henry!" cried Mrs. Collinson, her handkerchief falling to the floor. "It worked!"

Collinson reached past her and took the electric coils. He pressed them to his chest.

The room danced crazily in electric light for a moment as

Kwame writhed on the floor, trying to regain his feet, and Collinson closed his eyes as the coils pumped electricity into his chest-box.

After a long moment he dropped the coils and looked at her. Her smile as he reached for her was the stuff of dreams.

"Be in me. Forever."

"Dinna be… a silly cow," managed Kwame as she took his hand and he lifted her. "Nothin' good ever came… ae… weird loony talk like that…"

But they were gone.

"This is turning out to be… quite the peculiar… turn of events," said Goldsworth, dabbing a handkerchief to his bloodied nose.

"Aye, an' haven't ye got a talent for fuckin' understatement?" snapped Kwame, picking up his gun. "Shite, has the dizzy bitch nae read a horror book? Fuckin' steamware-nightmare corpse barges in the room spoutin' sinister romantic phrases… ye run the other way."

"Perhaps she's not as lettered as you clearly are," said Goldsworth acidly. "In any event, we may want to save the literary analysis for after we've prevented the reanimated corpse from gutting his poor deluded wife."

"Sarcasm is very unbecomin' on ye, Avery."

"Egads, man, just give your mouth a godsdamn rest and let's after them!"

"Where?"

"Where else would she store two large resonant transformer circuits?"

"On the fuckin' moon? Like I've a clue —"

"For such a clever man, you really are considerably stupid. Let's to my quarters first. I've a plan."

"In case shootin' the bastard tae death doesnae work?"

"Yes. In case that sterling plan doesn't work on the electrically charged corpse that, and I really believe this is worth pointing out, is already dead."

"All right, Avery. Keep ye knickers on."

They arrived in the cargo hold too late.

The transformer circuits were not overly difficult to find; the aft recesses of the gloomy hold were alive with the spitting coils arcing their deadly charges.

"Reckon they're over there?"

"Yes, Kwame. Yes, I do."

The two of them sprinted the two hundred metres, Kwame's pistol in hand and Goldsworth's pince-nez firmly in place, as the coils built to a sparking crescendo.

They framed Collinson, the electricity crackling over his smoking suit as he dropped his wife's body. One hand held a wickedly sharp scalpel; in the other he held her heart, still beating in time with the jolts of electricity.

His eyes, the dead one and the fresh one both, fell on them.

"Aim for the box," suggested Goldsworth.

"Ye dinna need to tell me twice."

"So aim for the godsdamn box!"

Kwame lifted his pistol and fired five shots as Collinson started forward. Four of them slammed into the steamware box bolted into his flesh; Collinson came on undeterred.

"We shall be. As one. For all time. She. In me."

"Save the loony talk for ye dead wife —" managed Kwame before a heavy fist slammed into his chest. The blow cracked something and he sailed backwards, toppling a stack of crates. Glassy pain exploded in his chest.

"Kwame, the —" began Goldsworth, and then Collinson was on him.

"I. In you."

He slammed the scalpel into Goldsworth's chest.

Kwame pulled himself up drunkenly as Goldsworth screamed. His chest flared in protest every time he drew breath. His gun was gone.

"Hey, ye ugly bastard!" he bellowed, the effort bringing the pain in his chest to an excruciating peak. "That the only way ye could think tae keep hold ae her, eh? There's no way she'd give ye her heart the traditional way any more, eh? Nae wi' a face looks like someone stuck it in a fuckin' airship engine, ye grim-looking cunt!"

Collinson let go of Goldsworth and turned.

"She. In me." Collinson held up the heart and looked at with something like love.

"It goes better the other way around, mate. This won't be the first time I've broken a heart or two." He lifted his hand up. "I found my gun."

Collinson's eyes snapped to him.

"No."

"Fuckin' yes." He pulled the trigger.

The heart exploded with a wet smack, showering Collinson with chunks of gory muscle.

Collinson howled with anguish and rage, his ruined face contorting into a snarl, and he charged.

"Shit shit shit ye'd best nae be dead Goldsworth, ye wee shite!" yelled Kwame as he tumbled to the ground and under the legs of the charging monster.

Goldsworth, his shirt slick with blood, reached into his jacket and feebly tossed Kwame the gun.

He rolled onto his back as he caught the weapon, Collinson towering over him again and those hard fists coming down —

The rail gun gave a sharp hiss, electric tendrils curling down its barrel, and the steam-box imploded. A fraction of a second later the rail-charged round punched through his back and the high ceiling with a harsh smack.

The walking corpse blinked once, twice, and he tottered over Kwame, abject surprise etched into his ruined features.

"Together." He lurched away from Kwame, his twice-dying eyes fixed on his wife. He stumbled, fell, crawled on. "Forever. Together. For…"

He fell again. Couldn't quite pull himself up. A moment later, he stopped altogether.

"How far… did ye say them rail rounds go… again?" said Kwame through gritted teeth, waves of white-hot pain radiating from his chest.

"Far…" said Goldsworth, his face sweat-sheened.

"Hope I didnae… hit anyone… on the way up…"

"Concern… for your fellow… man?" Goldsworth managed to get his eyelids to half-mast and smiled faintly. "There's hope… for you… yet…"

The sound of shouting and footsteps came.

"Get a doctor!" Kwame stumbled to Goldsworth's side and fell to his knees. "Dinna worry, ye… soft shite. Help's comin'."

"I fear it… may be… a tad late."

"Dinna be daft. Jes' a tick."

Goldsworth grasped his hand with surprising strength, took it in his other, squeezed.

"You are… the best of… men, Mr. Asseri," he said as the doctor arrived and pulled his shirt open. "I pray… you live to see… equality for your people. I… shouldn't think… I shall."

"Ye'll be right, Avery, eh?" said Kwame with a weak smile. "S' jes' a flesh wound, right?" Dinna be soft."

"I am… proud… to have made… your acquaintance, Kwame. Now I… go… into that good… light." He coughed feebly. "Farewell."

Kwame clapped his hands over Goldsworth's and lowered his head.

"Aye, ye daft bugger. Aye. I'll be seein' —"

"It's just a flesh wound," said the doctor, removing his stethoscope. "He'll be fine."

Kwame looked at him. "Wha'?"

Goldsworth opened his eyes again.

"Oh."

Epilogue

"I'll tell ye this much, Captain," said Kwame on the bridge, his face set. A heavy bandage ringed his chest. "Collinson may have escaped detection for two days. He may have murdered John Downes' an'took his eye. He may have disembowelled Airman Peters. He may even have managed to cut his wife's heart oot after abductin' her. But —" Kwame stopped and considered this. "Actually, aye. He pulled off everythin' he was after doin'. Fucked up a bit there, didn't we?"

"Yes, Mr. Asseri," replied the captain, a thickset man with a trimmed salt-and-pepper beard. "I'd be inclined to agree."

"Hey — at least we made the fucker suffer before we put him down, eh? I shot his wife's heart in front ae 'im. Didn't half piss him off."

"Yes. You also put a hole in the balloon that prevents us all from plummeting ten thousand feet at any one time," said the captain coldly. "And you killed a personal friend of mine. And slept with his wife."

"Oh. Ye heard about that."

"Legally, you are inculpable. The duel was above board. Lady Grosvenor is free to make whatever ill-advised, grossly inappropriate personal choices she desires. I commissioned Mr. Goldsworth to find and stop the murderer, and he consequently contracted you."

"Aye, that's all true."

"You are therefore free to go. You will get the hell off my ship as soon as we make berth in Three Pines."

"Nae worries, pal, I'll be ootae ye hair in no time, eh?"

"Get off my bridge, you murdering, philandering animal."

"Aye. Pleasure tae finally meet ye, Captain."

"Avery, ye soft shite," said Kwame with a chuckle, shaking the recumbent scientist's hand. "Ye're nae gonna start blubbin' like a baby again, are ye?"

"I shouldn't think so," said Goldsworth sheepishly. "It was the fear of death talking, you know."

"Oh aye, all that stuff about me bein' 'the best ae men'. Think I'll get that framed."

"We got him, Kwame. We got the bastard."

"Aye. We didnae actually figure anythin' oot in time or prevent the murder of any of the people he was wantin' tae kill, like, but we made the bastard hurt."

"When you put it like that, you make it sound like abject failure."

"Ah, well. I pulled my weight. Ye've my coin, I take it?"

Goldsworth frowned. "Straight to business, what? I'm not exactly in a position to fetch you your coin now, Kwame. It's in my quarters."

"Aye, nae worries. I'll see myself in."

"You don't have a key."

"Aye. Doesnae usually stop me." Kwame sketched a salute. "I'll be seein' ye, Avery. I'm away when we dock in Three Pines."

"You're not going to say good-bye?"

"Nah. There's a bottle ae brandy wi' my name on it, an' a certain widow clamourin' tae see me 'fore I'm off."

"You won't steal anything else from my quarters, will you? Kwame?" Goldsworth chuckled nervously. "Kwame?"

To his credit, he only stole an extra ten sovereigns.

Facing the Modern World
By Ray Dean

The normal bustle of the port was interrupted by a single man; feet braced shoulder width apart, a bowler set securely on the crown of his head. His richly colored skin spoke of a man accustomed to the touch of the sun. The smart suit of clothing did not fall from his shoulders like most suits, the dark grey pinstriped coat touched strong muscle where most would hang free. The captain gave him a wide berth, standing at the top of the gangplank with his boarding list pressed tightly to his chest. When the man turned to him, the Captain gave him a short nod of recognition and stiffened slightly as the man drew his feet together and bowed in reply.

It was only when the passenger had stepped onto the dock and moved toward the east that the Captain realized that he had been holding his breath. He'd carried Japanese to the Hawaiian Kingdom before, but those men were different. Their clothing rougher, the fabric, a serviceable weave that was meant for hard work. By the look of the wagons that met them at the docks, the men had work awaiting them on the sugar plantations in the Ewa area of Oahu.

This man, his soft footsteps moving him toward the thickest concentration of buildings in town, was not like the others. His purposeful strides made quick work of the distance and his head was held high, his chin lifted proudly away from his neck. If it wasn't for the difference in their language and the heathen beliefs of his people, the Captain reckoned that he might have consented to talk to him during the voyage. As it was, all he had call to do at this moment was to mark one more passenger off his list.

****

Traveling to the Hawaiian Kingdom had been a constant desire for Toshio since the grand visitation of King David Kalakaua in 1881. There had been few opportunities for him to speak to the monarch, but the few moments of time that Toshio gleaned during the official events had shown both men to be interested in many of the same interests.

Following the instructions leading him to the Palace there was little time to be distracted by his surroundings. Still, his eyes would drift up toward the wires strung from one tall post to another, pulled taut across each distance.

He had seen something similar in Japan before he left. The largest of the cities had small stretches of such cable and while he had hoped to see a demonstration he had yet to witness the marvel of denki, or electricity as the gaijin called it. The steam engines that created the energy, that brought mere wire to burn like the sun, fascinated Toshio. He'd seen drawings, read dispatches from Kyoto, but he had yet to see the flare of god-like energy bring daylight into the darkness.

The cables ran alongside the dirt road that was clearly marked on the hand-drawn map he held in his hands. The King's road was well traveled by foot and carriage. The distance from the harbor gave him time to rehearse the few Hawaiian words he had learned from Consul Irwin, the consul from Hawaii. When he reached the gates of the Palace he met the stern eyes of the guard beneath the stiff brim of his pristine white sun helmet and asked to speak with His Majesty.

****

The steward approached the gate with care. He had not travelled with King Kalakaua on his tour of the world but he had heard stories of the men of Japan. He'd heard of the samurai and the accounts gave him no small amount of pause. He expected a man in pants so big they could be considered skirts, a sword affixed to his hip, and a slick top-knot of hair pulled to the high point of his head.

When he finally stopped at the gate, safely between two of His Majesty's guards, he was quite taken aback by the picture before him. The man was dressed in a sober suit of brown, laced leather shoes and a proper bowler that might, if he wished to lean from one side to the other to see, hide the famed top-knot of a samurai warrior.

Tightening the reigns on his control and curiosity, the retainer inquired, "What is your business, sir?"

Beneath his solid stance, his feet shifted slightly toward each other as he bent at the waist. "I request an audience with His Majesty, King Kalakaua."

The retainer pondered the man's words as he affected a bow hoping to approximate the solemnity of the man's address. "His Majesty has no time to speak to you today." With a turn of his hand he indicated the Palace behind him at the center of the grounds. "He is in preparation for his birthday celebration.

Perhaps, in a few weeks after our guests have gone he may—"

"If you please," withdrawing a slip of paper from the inside breast pocket of his coat, the Japanese gentleman's earnest expression had an effect on the steward, "be so kind as to show His Majesty this paper."

The steward reached out to take the paper from his hand, shocked at the seemingly simple request.

"I will wait here." His message delivered, he stepped back away from the gate and set his feet apart in what seemed to be his customary stance.

The steward waited for a moment before shaking himself into action. He advanced a few steps and paused only when his nose came dangerously close to the iron bars. "If you please," he echoed the other man's words, "is there a name that I may give to his Majesty?"

His hands touched lightly near his hips on the upper part of his thighs, the visitor bowed his head slightly in answer. "Toshio," he remained bowed, "Nagata, Toshio."

****

Nearly an hour later, when the sun had begun its descent toward the Waianae Mountains, a rustle of movement heralded an answer from the King. When Toshio raised his head he was pleasantly surprised to see the very man standing before him. Averting his eyes and executing a deep bow, he spoke in a hushed and reverent tone, "Your Majesty."

"Come, Toshio-san."

The King's words may have shocked the guards, but their faces showed no reaction. No, it was the retainer, who had paused a foot or two behind his King, who showed his surprise plainly on his face. "But, Your Majesty, your birthday preparations—"

"Will continue without me for now." Aside from the staid and regal expressions of his official portraits, King David Kalakaua had an easy manner as he waved at the guards to get them to hurry as they opened the heavy wrought iron gates. When they were opened wide enough the Merrie Monarch* gestured for his guest to enter the Palace grounds.

The King bent his head to speak with his retainer as they strolled along. The smaller man hurried alongside the King, nodding over and over. They skirted along the side of the Palace and it was there that the King paused, allowing his retainer to rush on toward a smaller building near the wall at the corner. As the smaller man disappeared inside, the King gestured to the tree that stood before them. "This tree and this Palace," he opened his other hand toward the stately stone structure to their right, "I wonder... which will outlast the other."

Toshio thought over the issue and nodded in reply. "A truly interesting question, Your Majesty." He wondered aloud, "Only time will tell."

A door in the smaller structure swung open and a group of servants appeared, carting a table and chairs, trays of food and drink, and a small writing desk with an ink pot and a fluttering stack of pagers. They set up the appealing scene beneath the very tree that the two had considered. "Come and sit," the King urged Toshio to join him, "let us enjoy the shade from this monkeypod tree while we can."

Servants added the finishing touches as they approached the table situated near the base of the thick trunk. Pristine linen napkins curled elegantly below the edges of fine china. The chairs prepared for them were marked with the same elegantly gilded KK of the King's monogram.

The King was seated first and while Toshio settled himself into a chair, the monarch examined the drawing that his guest had brought with him. His lips curled in a curious smile. "I wondered where I left this."

The samurai, in the English-cut suit, was nearly smiling as well. "I found it beneath a table in Consul Irwin's office after your final visit."

Nodding, the monarch smiled. "That was our first meeting, Toshio-san." He looked at the paper one more time. "And now it has brought you across the ocean to us."

Toshio nodded. "I believe," his eyes rested on the nearby retainers for a moment, "that we may share some of the same concerns, Your Majesty."

With a wave the retainers and the servants disappeared into the adjacent building.

"And I believe, we have much to discuss." Putting the paper on the table between them, the King smoothed his broad tanned fingers over the pencil sketch. "Our Kingdoms," he began, "share some of the same... concerns in regards to defense."

"The Emperor agrees. Admiral Perry's arrival in our harbor clearly illustrated how ill-prepared we were to face a modern world."

The thought was a sobering one, the Hawaiian Kingdom had suffered a similar experience when they had, for a period of a few months, lost their independence to the British. It was only through the intervention of Admiral Thomas that the reins of governing had been restored to King Kamehameha III.

"What we lack," continued Toshio, his eyes watchful for the impact of his words on the Hawaiian rule, "are Navies of sufficient size and firepower and a cadre of commanders to ready our sailors to defend our islands."

"And yet," Kalakaua picked up the idea, "my inquiries have yielded little. For these nations that come to us with their treaties and trade agreements, they show little interest in selling us the ships to meet them as equals."

"They refuse, for they know, that if we have the ships to face them, we will would present more of a challenge than they would wish."

Toshio's wry tone was not lost on the Monarch."Yes," his dark eyes sparkled with merriment, "and yet they worry that we will let their refusals stymie our interest in such defensive preparations."

The samurai nodded in thanks as a servant poured him some fragrant tea. "If we are not allowed a Navy to defend our shores," he measured his words into a rhythm that allowed himself to consider his words from many perspectives before he voiced them, "we must find other ways to... deter an act of aggression from a foreign nation."

The King lifted his own cup into his large hands. "We," he also considered his words very carefully, "are not in favor of a blatant show of force. My people wish for a peaceful existence, and I," he nodded," want the same." He took a sip of the brew and paused to savor the taste. "Guns lined along the harbor, on the wall of our Fort, are not the impression that we wish to present to the world." Gone was the merry look that had greeted Toshio at the gate. Now, he could see the heavy press of responsibility on the shoulders of this stately man. "I want to protect my people, Toshio-san, but I do not wish to cause fear by displaying the method of their protection like a," he gestured toward the steeple of the nearby St. Andrew's Cathedral, "gargoyle above their heads."

Toshio nodded as he thought through the King's words. While they shared some knowledge of each other's native tongues, with topics as dear and worrisome as this one, they were both interested in choosing their words as carefully as they could.

"And you brought my drawing to me."

"Yes, Your Majesty," Toshio shifted slightly in his chair, "I believe I understand what this represents." Pointing to the drawing, a shape that resembled a fish with an oddly shaped tail, puffs of air trailing behind its slim body. "A torpedo, Your Majesty. A modern torpedo that propels itself rather than sitting idly in place waiting to realize its purpose."

They shared a smile. "Yes... one that is fueled by a boiler much like the numerous vessels that arrive on our shores each day. If the power of steam can bring such wonders to our shores," the King surmised, "than then the power can also be used to protect ourselves from the very same technology."

Setting his cup down on its saucer, the King reached for a powdered sweet from a nearby tray. "While the idea fills me with wonder," he continued, "I can not think of a way to direct it to its chosen destination."

Using his breath to cool the surface of the tea, Toshio observed the ripples of the liquid against the far side of the cup. "Perhaps the current is the answer, Your Majesty."

The King lifted his curious gaze to the warrior seated before him. "How so?"

"The current," repeated Toshio, "my father and many generations before him fished the waters near our village. There They were as familiar to those in my village as the pathways and the roads on land."

King Kalakaua smiled, a dawning of hope came across his features. "The same can be said of my people; the Kanaka maoli know the currents with equal familiarity." He tilted his head slightly to watch the curving path of Toshio's finger along the paper, following the gentle curve of the fish-like torpedo. "We will find a way to emulate the movement of a fishtail, allowing the torpedo to swim the currents to the harbor."

"The ships," Toshio's thoughts continued along the same path, "with their wide girth and heavy cargos will be easy targets." He cupped his hands in imitation of the deep curve of the Navy ships in the water. "The depth they reach is unlike that of our smaller native vessels."

"Yes," agreed the King, "if our little fish were to swim deep in the channels, riding the currents beneath the hulls of our own vessels, we would have little fear of affecting those friendly to our nations."

They would have continued on from there but the King's retainer stepped out onto the porch of the house with a strained look pulled across his features. "Your Majesty, Queen Kapiolani requests that you adjourn to the Palace and begin preparations for the evening's festivities."

"Yes," the King lifted himself from the chair and nodded at the retainer and Toshio in turn, "I will, but I ask you to join us tonight, my friend." Workmen rounded the corner of the Palace and the Monarch gestured to them. "Tonight, we shall celebrate my birthday with a grand party." The power lines that had stretched along the King's road also led up to the stone Palace. "We shall light the night sky with our own fire, Toshio-san. Electricity has come to our Palace, before that of the Americans' own White House. You, my friend, will be a part of our celebration as we join the modern world in fine style."

The two men, born thousands of miles away from each other, bonded now by a love for their own homelands and the curious thrill of science, stood and reached their hands across the short distance between them and clasped their hands in friendship. "Together," ventured Toshio, "we will create this torpedo together."

"Together" agreed the King, his hand returning the warm embrace of his friend, "Then we shall no longer fear the threat of foreign ships in our harbors."

United in their aims, they released each other's hands and began to part, but a shadow slipped down from the roof of the Palace and ate up the ground between that stately structure and the leafy arbor of their meeting place. Shielding their eyes from the vestiges of the late afternoon sun they both looked into the sky and felt their tanned complexions pale.

High above the King's Palace blotting out the sanguine blush of the approaching sunset, a large barrel-chested ship floated through the sky. The impact of this sighting sent thrills through their bodies, and seared fear through their veins. Now, as they began work on a defense to protect their nations' waters, they would have to worry about the skies over their heads.

An Honest Ulster Spinner
By Seamus Sweeney

Margaret's foot kept a steady rhythm on the wheel. A year or so before, she had begun to notice an ache in her right knee and ankle during the first few hours of spinning each morning. The ache would steadily grow until reaching a near-unbearable intensity, but then would suddenly subside. She found that distributing her weight slightly reduced the duration of this pain, but it was now the few hours after work that became ones of agony. Thank the Lord that Caroline was now of an age to cook and help with the wains. Margaret hadn't wanted to keep her from the schoolhouse, though Caroline—dear child!—was eager to help. She had always been a kind and affectionate girl, and since Robert had gone and not returned, had become a second mother to her brothers.

Every Sabbath, on the way to and from the meeting-house Margaret walked straight ahead, keeping her gaze steady. A year before, just before the pain began, Robert had gone to Belfast to get work in the factories fabricating Computation Engines. They had heard nothing of him since.

As she spun Margaret could see right out the cottage door, to the hills that faced the sea. It would be worth it, she thought as she often did, to get enough money to give Caroline a dowry that would keep her on the land, a farmer's wife. And Then to settle the boys somewhere, maybe on their sister's new farm if it was big enough, maybe for one of them to become a minister and do the Lord's work. Caroline wouldn't have to spin, Margaret would think, not that spinning is a sin she would immediately add to herself.

A few minutes earlier, Caroline, not yet fourteen, had left the cottage with the older boys to walk them to the schoolhouse, holding little John's hand as she did so. John was too small for any schooling. It was a little past nine, and Margaret had already been spinning, pressing on the wheel again and again with her right foot, adjusting the loom every so often with her hands, for four hours. Around now, the pain would usually stop.

She would stop at ten for a break, some potato cake and tea from the range, and then spin for another six hours. When the wains came back she would settle them with Caroline, keeping a sober countenance through the pain, and then while they slept spin three more hours. Every Friday afternoon the Canister Men would come, with their sleek black carriage, and take the canisters she had spun, hand over a few coins, and move on. This money, aside from a desultory few eggs from the chickens the children tended under Caroline's supervision, was the family's sole income.

Where had Robert gone? No one had heard. Belfast was a little over fifty miles away, if you could fly over Lough Neagh, but for those left in the cottages in the townland, it may as well have been America. In every cottage their size, the men had gone to work in the fabricating mills, where the energy spun in cottages and crofts all over Ulster could be converted into Computational Power. What a Babbage Engine fully loaded with Spun Energy Canisters would do, neither the spinners at their wheels nor the workmen in their factories were told.

Margaret would tell herself that she never wondered. Robert had gone. He had lived with them, a hard worker, a proper husband, a father neither too severe nor too lax, and then he was gone. She had six children by him, and buried two, the two boys born after Caroline. He had gone to Belfast to work, as he had gone to big farms by the Bann to work other winters, but this time there was no word and no return. They had been married fifteen years, years she looked back at as steady, respectable time, when the future was laid out as serenely as the hills she could see through the cottage door. Margaret would catch herself wondering and say to herself, stop, woman, do not question the fate that has befallen you, you know that you have done no wrong, you can walk with your head held high.

Margaret also told herself she never wondered what the canisters engines were for. She would tell herself to be thankful for the Lord had provided labour for her hands. Her father had been a spinner, for in his day men spun as much as women, and the work came easy to her. If her mind sometimes wondered what transpired, in Belfast, or in Bristol, or in Glasgow, or in Liverpool, or in London, or on the fields of battle all over the Empire, when the Babbage Engine was loaded with the Canisters which she and thousands of Ulsterwomen working in cottages for a few coins had spun full of energy, she would tell herself to focus on the work, on pressing at a steady rate and making the shuttle dance.

Margaret was from a few miles outside Dungannon, far from here, and in Robert's absence made sure not to betray his memory or her own home place in any way. Gossip made its way into even these parts, to congregations leaving the meeting houses and to the parents waiting for their children to finish Sunday School, and while she avoided all unnecessary talk, Margaret overheard tales of men alone in Belfast pressed into the ravenous navy of Her Majesty, stretched as it was by the massive victories the Empire was winning thanks to the Babbage Engine. They were all loyal subjects of Her Majesty Queen Victoria, and news of the Fall of Rome to her armies, coming so soon after the conquest of the French and reconquest of the Americas, made it easy to believe that the Lord was on the side of Queen. Had she not humbled that Anti-Christ, the Pope of Rome?

That morning she did not have to work to banish such distracting thoughts from her mind. The rhythm of the work was better than it had been for some months. She felt the pain vanish from her earlier than usual, without reaching its usual crescendo. These mornings the repetition of the movements involved brought Margaret a sense of being detached from all around her, being detached from time, from the cottage, from the fields and drumlins around, from the green earth itself.

Caroline came in, still holding John's hand. As they called in greeting, Margaret suddenly felt a rending pain, seeming to start in her lower back and to go on to tear her entire right side. She stood up, then felt a deeper agony run through her. All her weight crumpled her body onto the pedal, and the sudden presence of sustained pressure shot off the canister, her morning's work was gone. Margaret realised, as Caroline sped to her side, that there was only one thing she could do.

"Mam! You're hurted!" said Caroline.

"It is nothing, child. Carry you me to the seat there yonder by the fire."

Caroline did so, supporting her mother with little John's earnest help. When she was seated, Margaret felt the pain seeming to reach a duller but constant pitch. "It is nothing, girl, just a little turn. I will be aright for the spinning soon."

There was a pause. Margaret felt the pain continue. She thought of the now empty canister, and the pile in the parlour she needed to fill for the following Friday. She tried to keep the weight out of her next words: "Caroline, d'ye think you could spend a session on the spinner?"

Caroline, of course, was eager to assent, and having watched her mother knew exactly what was to be done. With little John cradled in his mother's arms, she watched her daughter spin, and Margaret repeated to herself over and over again, it is only for today, it is only for today, only for today, only for today.

Stolen Cargo
By Nicole Lavigne

Althea looked up at the helium balloon tethered above the airship and suppressed a shudder. Her hand trembled as she brought the champagne glass to her lips. She downed it. She exchanged the empty glass for a fresh one off a server's tray and assembled a smile over her clenched teeth.

She turned as her husband's voice rang out over the crowd from large speaker boxes spaced around the deck.

"Welcome ladies and gentlemen," said Hastings Cartwright. "Thank you all for joining us on this special occasion. Airships are the ideal form of travel." He laughed. "Though I'll admit I might be a little biased as London's top producer of them."

Laughter enveloped Althea.

"It takes dozens of highly trained men working together in perfect synchronicity to successfully drive an airship and a single misstep can lead to disaster. But not anymore. Ladies and gentlemen, tonight you have the pleasure of experience the flight of the world's first automaton airship." He paused for effect.

Althea's eyes roamed over the guests. Most were murmuring to each other in excitement or awe. A man quirked one red eyebrow. He wore a well-made business suit but didn't quite blend in with the rest of the socialites. His eyes met hers and Althea recognized him as her husband's competitor, Ceddrik Donnally. She turned her attention back to her husband.

"Thanks to the tireless work of Dr. Oswell Baxter," he pointed to a short red-haired man at the front of the crowd, "this airship is completely voice controlled, tuned in to its captain, and commands can be given from any position on the ship, simply by addressing the ship itself." Hastings paused.

"Garrett, give us a tour of London."

Althea's heart stopped. Garrett? Her breath came in shallow gasps. She gulped back the rest of her champagne while fighting back tears of grief and anger. A hum rose from the bowels of the ship. Ropes detached themselves from their moors and slithered back into the ship, coiling themselves away. The ramp raised itself and slid underneath the deck. Althea's stomach lurched as the airship rose into the air. She reached for the railing and clutched it so hard her fingertips went numb.

"Welcome to the future!"

Her husband's voice was distant behind the wall of cheers. She jumped when he kissed her cheek.

"Smile darling," he whispered in her ear. "This is our big day. A time to celebrate."

Rage pushed her terror back. She focused on his face. "Celebrate? Should I celebrate how you abused the memory of our son?"

"Hush. I did this in his honour; to avoid such tragic accidents happening to someone else. We are creating a better world."

"A world in which our son would have no place."

"I wouldn't be so sure about that darling."

Althea frowned at him.

"Come with me. I have something to show you that I think might change your mind about all of this."

****

Althea's pounding heart descended from her throat as her husband led her down into the ship. Now it churned in her stomach instead of choking her. She focused on Hasting's heels. From the corner of her eyes she glimpsed opulent dining rooms, lounges, and guest quarters.

The lower they descended, the less finished the spaces were. "We're a little behind schedule," he said. "Nothing major, just the finishing touches, and nothing that needed to delay our demonstration." She made no comment.

The third floor down was closed off by a large, steel door. The floor under them vibrated and Althea could hear the loud hum and whir of machines. Hastings pulled a ring of keys from his pocket and unlocked the door. Lights turned on automatically as he led her down a hallway and into a large room.

Rows of large jars sat on long tables with wires connecting them to turning gears or dials. Her feet slowed as she passed the first set of jars. She peered into one on table labeled 'climate control.' When her mind finally made sense of the grey mass floating inside, bile rose in her throat. She had to bend over and breathe carefully to keep from throwing up her champagne. Brains. Each jar contained a brain floating in liquid.

"Come on, there's more."

Althea looked up at her husband. He was beaming at her with pride. Did he not understand how horrifying this was? She followed him, trying very hard not to look at, or think about, the brains and to keep her breathing slow and steady.

Hastings led her to the far end of the room. A single jar sat on the large station cluttered with gauges and wires. A gramophone protruded from the station with a speaker box beside it.

"Isn't it beautiful?"

"It's an abomination!"

"Would you say that to your son?"

Althea gaped at him.

Hastings turned towards the gramophone. "Say hello to your mother, Garrett."

A hollow, mechanical voice emitted from the speaker on the station.

"Hel-lo Mo-ther."

"You named this... this thing after our son?"

Hastings smiled condescendingly. "No darling," he pointed to the brain on the station, "this is our son."

"That's impossible." Althea shook her head as tears rolled down her cheeks. "Our son is dead!"

"No. Don't you see? I saved our son. I saved all these people." He gestured to the other brains in the room. "They were dying. I gave them life, purpose. They would have been rotting in the ground."

Althea shivered. She felt empty. "How?"

"Garrett was dying. I was able to save him, his brain, before he died."

Her tears stopped. "You told me he died in the hospital. You lied to me? What if he could have recovered? You killed our son!"

She beat on his large chest with her fists. Hastings did not try to stop her. After a moment he gently reached his arms around her, hushing her. Althea pushed him back.

"No! Don't touch me."

He scowled down at her.

"Take a few moments to speak with Garrett. You'll see. The chances of him recovering were almost nonexistent, the doctors made that clear. This is what he wanted. Ask him. But don't take too long; we have guests to entertain upstairs. Tidy yourself up and join us, before they start to worry."

He kissed her cheek and walked down the long hall. Althea glared after him. When he was gone she turned to the station. The sight of the brain nauseated her. She focused instead on the gramophone and speaker.

"Garrett? Is that really you?"

"Yes."

Althea shuddered at the mechanical sound. "It can't be. This can't be real."

"It is true Mo-ther."

"How do I know it's really you?"

"Do you re-mem-ber when I was a boy, you read to me ev-er-y night, al-ways the same stor-y. I dreamed of fly-ing. You were so proud when I be-came a pi-lot. You cried with joy. Fa-ther wan-ted me to work with him on the air-ships. I did not. That night, I asked you to read me that stor-y a-gain."

Althea sniffled. "I remember. Oh Garrett." She reached out and ran her fingers on the wood top of the station. "I'm so sorry Garrett."

"Is it true? Did you really want to be like this?"

"It was the on-ly way."

She wiped a tear from her eye. "I suppose, you're still here at least."

"No."

"What?"

"This is no life. I feel no-thing, on-ly the ship that I con-trol. I can ne-ver fall in love and mar-ry. Look at what Fa-ther has done. So ma-ny peo-ple, so ma-ny lives de-stroyed pre-ma-ture-ly for Fa-ther's gain. I love you Mo-ther, but I would ra-ther be dead than con-ti-nue like this."

Tears cascaded down her cheeks again. "I'm sorry, Garrett. I wish there was a way that I could make things right again."

"Help me stop him be-fore he hurts more peo-ple. That was the on-ly rea-son I a-greed to this, so I could have a chance to stop him."

Althea took a step back. "I'm sorry Garrett. I... I have to get back up to the guests."

She turned.

"Please Mo-ther," the mechanical voice called after her. She ran from the room.

****

Music and voices drifted down from the deck to where Althea

sat, unmoving, in the stairwell.

"Mrs. Cartwright?"

Althea looked up through a daze into Dr. Baxter's familiar blue eyes and greyed hair.

"Mrs. Cartwright, your husband asked that I come check on you and make sure that you made it back up to the party alright."

He looked down at her.

"Yes, it quite takes my breath away, too. The things that we have been able to accomplish, the ability to maintain brain function separate from the body, it's remarkable isn't it? I am particularly proud of our success with your son. Most of the others have limited capabilities, but your son is a unique specimen. We were fortunate to recover his brain before his injuries caused any further damage."

"You were the one who did this to him?"

"Oh yes, I performed all of the surgeries personally. It's very tricky work. I could not risk anyone else making mistakes and losing a specimen, especially not with the position of honour that your husband had planned for Garrett. He is not merely a pilot now, he commands the entire ship."

He smiled down at her.

"But I will have to train others to perform the operation in order to reach the production levels Hastings is planning."

Althea choked down the lump in her throat. "What production levels?"

"We are planning to make a whole fleet of automaton airships.

We truly are changing the world."

Althea's heart began to race. More ships. More people violated. More children stolen from their mothers, losing their lives like her Garrett.

He smiled down at her. "We should really go back up now Mrs. Cartwright. The guests have begun inquiring about your absence and these floors are still a disgraceful mess, no place for a lady such as yourself." He cast a disapproving eye at the tools on the floor beside her.

He turned to head back upstairs. She felt only steel in her hand as cold as her skin, the weight of the wrench as she swung. Her arm jolted when the wrench connected. There was a loud crack. Dr. Baxter fell. She stared at him lying limp on the floor.

What have I done? She reached towards him. Her hand recoiled. She ran back down the stairs, still clutching the wrench.

****

Althea ran past the rows of brains. She collapsed in front of the command station, sobbing.

"Garrett! What have I done?"

"What is it Mo-ther? What is wrong? Are you al-right?"

"I... I hit the Doctor."

"Is he a-live?"

"I don't know," she cried. "What if I killed him?"

"Do not wor-ry a-bout that now."

"They are going to do it again, Garrett. He said they are going to build more ships like this. They are going to hurt more people like they hurt you."

"Not if you stop them Mo-ther."

"I don't know how."

"De-stroy the ship."

"How? Can't you do something?"

"No. Fa-ther pro-grammed safe-ty pro-to-cols. I can-not de-stroy it my-self."

"Then what am I supposed to do?"

"De-stroy the brains. The ship can-not fly with-out them."

Althea looked down at the wrench in her hand, at the smudge of red on it. Althea stood up and walked towards the nearest of the brains. She grasped the handle of the wrench with both hands and screamed as she smashed the first jar. She turned to the next jar, smashing it as well. She continued down the row, hitting them one by one.

A loud clunking noise came from under the floor. The ship lurched, knocking Althea to the ground. She stood and smashed the next jar.

"Good. De-stroy them all."

A moment later Hastings came running in. "Althea, did you see what happened to Dr. Ba-" He stopped dead when he saw Althea.

"What are you doing?"

Althea ignored him.

"Althea, stop!" He grabbed her arm and pulled her away before she smashed another brain. Yanking the wrench from her hands, he threw it to the ground.

"What are you doing?" he roared.

"I can't let you do this! I won't let you hurt more people." She tried to pull away.

Hastings slapped her and she stopped struggling, staring at him shock.

"You will not get in my way. I will not allow you to jeopardize my work!"

"How da-"

The ship lurched to the side, throwing Althea and Hastings against the wall. She landed on top of him. Hastings hit his head. He groaned.

"Mo-ther. The ship is cra-shing. You must get off be-fore it is too late."

Althea crawled along the floor towards the door. When she reached it, she turned back to look at her husband. He was starting to stir. She looked away, facing the station that contained the remains of her son.

"Goodbye Garrett," she called. "I love you."

"I love you too, Mo-ther."

She stumbled out of the room.

As Althea stepped onto the deck, it tilted again. A woman screamed. People clung to the rails. Glasses crashed, spilling champagne across the floor. A loud rumbling sounded from under their feet, followed by a crash. Ceddrik approached her.

"Mrs. Cartwright, what is going?"

"Something is wrong with the ship. Hastings and Dr. Baxter are trying to deal with it but we need to get everyone off the ship."

He nodded. A grinding drew their attention to the rear of the airship. Trap doors opened in the floor and a small evacuation craft lifted from beneath. Ceddrik directed guests into the small craft. When it was filled, a red light blinked. Gears turned and belts transferred it out into the open air. Another rose to take its place. Althea and Ceddrik climbed into the second evacuation ship with the rest of the guests.

As they drifted towards the ground, Althea turned towards him. He fiddled with the control panel on the small craft.

"What are you doing?"

"You'll have to forgive me, but I don't trust these automated ships."

Althea laughed bitterly. "After today, I cannot blame you for that. Are you sure that's a good idea though?"

"I am your husband's top competitor; I know how to handle an aircraft." He looked back at the airship they had abandoned. "I hope that he and the doctor are able t-"

A loud explosion rocked them. The ball of fire that had been Hasting's airship heated Althea's face. She started to hyperventilate, gasping for breath as though the smoke from the ship were choking her across the distance. Ceddrik put a gentle hand on her back.

"Breathe. Put your head between your knees and just focus on breathing."

She did as he said. After a few moments her breathing returned to normal. She sat up, her eyes red and tears streaking her face.

"I am terribly sorry for your loss, madam."

Althea nodded. They sat in silence for a time, watching the

Printed in Great Britain
by Amazon.co.uk, Ltd.,
Marston Gate.